The Hidden Two

by

Kimberlee R. Mendoza

The Forgotten Ones, Book 3

The Hidden Two

Cover Art by *Kim Mendoza*

The Wild Rose Press, Inc.
PO Box 708
Adams Basin, NY 14410-0708
Visit us at www.thewildrosepress.com

Publishing History
First Crimson Rose Edition, 2018
Print ISBN 978-1-5092-2223-0
Digital ISBN 978-1-5092-2224-7

The Forgotten Ones, Book 3
Published in the United States of America

According to the BBC*, there are currently an estimated three hundred thousand child soldiers in the world, most in places like Sierra Leone, Liberia, Congo, Sudan, Sri Lanka, Afghanistan, and Burma.

For two decades in Uganda, ninety percent of the soldiers who fought in their various wars were children. Children are small and can infiltrate tight spaces undetected. Children seem innocent and are less likely to be a target. Children can be taught, blackmailed, and brainwashed. And in some cultures, children are unimportant and expendable.

In 1989, a former C.I.A. agent, Mel Greenstone returned from Africa with an epiphany for a black ops unit like none the U.S. Government had ever seen. However, he wasn't able to convince several high-ranking officials to implement his plan—to recruit orphans, homeless, and young criminals to a secret organization and train them as special agents. He decided to take matters into his own hands. With a few financial backers, he created S.I.U.—the Secret Intelligence Unit. In Greenstone's words, "Young people without a real future will be given one as the next generation of soldiers."

Years later, six of these soldiers fought back and imprisoned Greenstone, believing that the head of the snake had been cut off. Desiring a normal life on the run, they were determined to prove their freedom. Then they discovered S.I.U. still had a leader—Harding. With the help of many hands, they were able to take down S.I.U. and imprison their leader.

Dedication

To Ricky & Maddie
May you two have an amazing life together; love never
hidden, but always open and freely given in every
aspect of your home.

Prologue

According to the BBC*, there are currently an estimated three hundred thousand child soldiers in the world, most in places like Sierra Leone, Liberia, Congo, Sudan, Sri Lanka, Afghanistan, and Burma.

For two decades in Uganda, ninety percent of the soldiers who fought in their various wars were children. Children are small and can infiltrate tight spaces undetected. Children seem innocent and are less likely to be a target. Children can be taught, blackmailed, and brainwashed. In some cultures, children are unimportant and expendable.

In 1989, a former C.I.A. agent, Mel Greenstone returned from Africa with an epiphany for a black ops unit like none the U.S. Government had ever seen. However, he wasn't able to convince several high-ranking officials to implement his plan—to recruit orphans, homeless children, and young criminals to a secret organization and train them as special agents. He decided to take matters into his own hands. With a few financial backers, he created S.I.U.—the Secret Intelligence Unit. In Greenstone's words, "Young people without a real future will be given one as the next generation of soldiers."

Years later, six of these soldiers fought back and imprisoned Greenstone, believing the head of the snake had been cut off. Desiring a normal life, they were

1

determined to prove their freedom. Then they discovered S.I.U. still had a leader—Harding. With the help of many hands, they were able to take down S.I.U. and imprison its leader. Now, they are on a journey to discover the many souls who are still lost or forgotten.

*http://www.bbc.co.uk/worldservice/people/features/childrensrights/childrenofconflict/soldier.shtml

Chapter One

Teddy adjusted his weight on the back of the rooftop. It had been hours. His nose, hands, and dare he say, rear-end were cold and numb. Any longer and they would have to scrape him off the shingles.

Where are they? For probably the thirtieth time, he glanced in the binoculars. The landscape remained vacant. Unmoving. No sign of them. Laura had strictly said not to move until he saw...

Wait. Headlights. Through binoculars, he confirmed the make and model—yes, it was them. He slid off the roof and dropped to the open window below his perch. His tense muscles complained in revolt, but he couldn't stop. Not now. With a quick glance back to be sure, he ran for the stairs. "They're coming!"

"Everyone down," Laura hissed to team. The room fell into a hush. Only the sound from clock above the entryway echoed in the space. *Tick, tick, tick.* Someone's foot scraped on the floor, and a few jeered, "sshhh."

Outside, rocks crackled under car tires as the vehicle pulled into the driveway. There was a slight hesitation before the sound of doors opening and slamming; then, a duo of steps made their way to the front door.

Teddy tensed. His hands annoyingly sweaty, his

mouth super dry. This was it. He readied himself.

The handle jiggled. The door opened. The light popped on.

"Surprise!" everyone yelled.

Charlie and Eri stood in the doorway with complete awe on their faces. They glanced at each other and then back to the group.

A huge grin spread across Teddy's face to the point his cheeks hurt. He couldn't help it. They were back—married. Crazy things kept happening. Happy things. It had been almost eight months since Laura had plucked him from Hell, and now, everything just kept getting better and better. It consumed him with joy. He ran to Charlie and Eri and hugged them both, probably a bit too tight.

Charlie politely pushed back and smiled.

"Teddy, what is all this?" Eri asked.

"It's a party for you, of course." Teddy smiled and threw his arms out wide to encompass the room.

"A party? Why?" Eri looked at him with a coy smile.

"Please." Teddy rolled his eyes. "A party for our two friends, who thought they did a secret thing, but come on, we *knew*. We knew you got married, because well…we are all spies, after all. It is hard to keep things like that from spies, because spies are smart and know things. You know this, so why even try?"

The two of them glanced at each other and laughed.

Laura stepped forward and hugged them both. "Congrats, my friends. And Teddy is right; you can't keep secrets from us."

"Why you did it in private is a bit unclear," Myers

said, stepping forward to shake Charlie's hand. "We're family. Not cool."

"But we aren't about to let you avoid a chance for us to spoil you with a reception." Teddy beamed. "Bryce and Deshawn did the cooking. Willow did the cake. I decorated. Not bad, right?"

Eri and Charlie glanced round the room and laughed. White and silver streamers were everywhere, complimented by mylar balloons. It looked more like a tacky '80s prom than a wedding reception, but Teddy didn't care. He liked what he did.

"So, *why* did you elope?" Laura asked, folding her arms in front of her. "Myers is right. We're family."

The two exchanged glances. Eri started to speak, but then stopped. Charlie responded, "We were just afraid that if we tried to have a regular wedding something would go wrong. Every happy moment is always stolen from us. It just felt better this way. Besides, Las Vegas is just a few hours from here."

"In other words, they had too much to drink the other night and did it on a whim," Deshawn joked.

"Precisely," Charlie said.

Eri elbowed him. "That's not true."

"Okay, fine." Charlie wrapped his arm around her shoulders and pulled her close. "I did it because I love her, and I didn't want to wait for the next bad guy to come and hurt us and not have done it."

Myers glanced at the floor, pain evident in his eyes. From what Teddy knew, that is precisely what happened to his girl, Denise. Laura must have noticed and gave him a side squeeze.

"I still think you could have invited us," Teddy said. It didn't make much sense to him. Myers was right. They were family and would want to share in that moment. Didn't they understand that? Oh well, he was happy for them. No one would ever put that couple together—the quiet, Chinese ninja with the long-haired, blond computer hack. Only God would make such a match.

"Well, I'm glad you're back in one piece. We were starting to get worried." Laura led them into the dining room of the condo to a large spread of T-bone steaks, twice-cooked potatoes, Caesar salad, cheddar biscuits, and a berry fruit salad. On the counter was the three-layer vanilla cake Willow had made, topped with two army men. One of the plastic soldiers had toilet paper stuck to the back of its head—Teddy's contribution.

"Alicia still isn't back, huh?" Eri said to the empty chair.

Teddy shook his head, shooting a glance across the table. He missed his friend, and Helena's downcast expression said she also missed her sister. Not once did Alicia indicate she wanted to leave. She seemed happy here. Possibly even happy with him. His mind glazed over to the last time he had seen her. Around two a.m., Teddy had heard someone or something moving around in the basement. He crept down the stairs with a kitchen knife, only to find Alicia tucked in the corner with a cell phone in her lap, sleeping. When she opened her eyes, she jumped up, ran into his arms, and kissed him passionately. It completely disarmed him. They had flirted, but never acted on it. His heart swelled, excited at the future they might have together. So much so, he didn't bother to ask what was wrong or why she was in the basement.

The next morning, she was gone. The only

evidence she had ever been there was a note stating she was sorry, but she wanted to go back to Puerto Rico. No other explanation.

Helena and several of them had looked for her for days but ended up with nothing. The trail was cold.

"I'm sorry, Teddy." Eri touched his shoulder.

Teddy blinked out of his memory and nodded. "Yeah."

"I'm sure she'll return eventually," Eri said.

Teddy hated the attention. It just made it hurt worse. "In the meantime, let's eat. Deshawn has been bragging about his steaks all day. I want to see if they live up to all the hype."

"Hey, man, they will. No doubt. My old man was a grill master." The black man wiped both his hands over his bald head, shrugging before holding his arms out to his sides. "It's in the DNA."

Everyone laughed.

Bryce said a blessing over the couple and the food, and then, they sat to eat.

"Myers," Charlie said, passing the biscuits, "Were you able to find out anything from that website I sent you?"

Myers shook his head. "I think it's a dead end."

Laura frowned. "At this point, I don't know if that is good news or bad news. No news could mean we found all of S.I.U., or it could mean they've hidden them really well. Either way, I think we need to let it go."

"Just because Myers has worn out his resources doesn't mean they aren't out there." Bryce took a bite of a strawberry and looked at Laura. "I don't want them creeping up on us again."

"I also don't want to kick over a hornets' nest like last time." Laura took a sip of her iced tea and glanced at Myers. It was no secret Laura felt responsible for Denise's death. The last time they went digging into S.I.U. was her call, and the group killed their friend for it.

"Honestly, I'm still trying to figure out why any of you think there are more?" Charlie lifted two potatoes onto his plate and passed the tray. "Why couldn't that be it? After all, we got Greenstone and Harding. An organization without a leader should fall. Am I right?"

Eri set her fork down and sighed. "He said he brought in over a hundred in just one year. That doesn't include the other people already out there. We've only rescued forty or so, and maybe shot another thirty. Where are the others? I really don't want to stop until we have saved all those kids. It's the right thing to do. We all know it."

Willow set her glass down and cleared her throat. "I know for a fact there are many more out there."

The table went silent as everyone looked at her.

"I know, because I helped recruit some of them. I may have been in jail for almost a year, but I was in the field for four more. At one point, we had close to a thousand soldiers around the globe."

Mouths visibly dropped. Teddy knew why. Most of them probably assumed she was a new recruit. When the team first met her, they guessed she was thirteen years old. Boy were they super surprised to find out she was actually twenty, just small in stature. Once they knew her age, Laura probably should have assumed she had been with S.I.U. for a while. The organization didn't often recruit older people.

"Why are you just telling us this now?" Laura asked with a tight smile.

"Mainly, I was scared. I've wanted to tell you, but you were shooting them."

By *them*, Teddy presumed she meant seasoned agents. He knew Willow when they were there, but only briefly. They were in different crews, and she was a few years older. He hadn't really thought about the fact she was a full-fledge agent.

Myers pushed back from the table and stood with steak knife in hand. "Do we have something to worry about here?"

"Sit down, Myers," Laura said. "We're not ruining the celebration."

Without taking his intense gaze from Willow, he sat back in the chair.

"I've proven I'm loyal to you." Willow glanced around the table. "You saw me. I was almost dead. I have harbored no positive feelings for the agency. I want to take them down as much as you do. Maybe more so."

The group all exchanged looks. Teddy believed her. But then, he believed everybody. It was his downfall. Overt optimism. "I say we trust her."

"I say we table this conversation until later," Helena said, then raised a glass. "To the happy couple. May the Lord bless them, and may they find their normal."

"To normal," everyone said in unison.

Chapter Two

Laura rolled over next to her husband and pulled the covers under her chin. His soft breathing said he was exhausted. If only her mind would shut down too. Not knowing Willow was a full agent disturbed her, especially since they would have been in the agency at the same time. Why had Laura never heard of her? Was she a spy meant to watch them?

Memories of finding her seemed to rule that out. When they found the frail red-headed girl, she looked close to death. She was quiet, almost shy. Instantly, Laura liked Willow and took the girl under her wing. Now, she was family.

"You okay?" Bryce said in the darkness.

"How can you tell?"

"A little over a year of marriage, I can tell when you're troubled by something."

She rolled over to face him, propping onto one elbow. "I just can't get the whole Willow thing out of my head."

Bryce slid back against the headboard and flipped on the lamp by his side. Dark hair, intense blue eyes, and firm jaw—he still took Laura's breath away. "Consider this. She was so malnourished and on the brink of death when we found her that I highly doubt she harbors any love for the agency."

Laura slid up next to him. "Then why did she lie to us?"

"Did she?"

That thought rolled around in her head over and over. *Did she?* Was not sharing information the same as lying? S.I.U. would instantly have an affirmative answer to that notion. It was hard for Laura to trust anyone, anyway; things like this got under her skin quickly, distorting any rational thoughts.

The sound of morning birds cooed in the distance reminding her it was late, or should she say early? She needed to sleep. Closing her eyes, she folded under Bryce's arm, into his chest, and tried to still her breathing.

He combed a hand through her short hair. "I don't think she lied to us. Maybe kept that from us, but can you really blame her? I say we give her the benefit of the doubt. She's been like family."

"I suppose you're right." She nodded toward the light on the nightstand. "We can sleep now."

"But you woke me up."

"So?"

A knowing grin slid across his lips.

She shook her head and laughed. "You know we need to sleep."

"Yes, eventually." He reached out and began to tickle her.

Someone knocked on the door. Both stopped and sat up.

"Yeah?" Laura said.

The door swung open, revealing a distraught Teddy. "Willow is gone."

"What do you mean gone?" Laura was instantly on

11

her feet, moving toward him.

Teddy backed into the hall and flipped on the light. "I mean, she was on the couch with us. I put her in her bed, covered her up. The pillow still has the indentation, and the covers are rumpled. She's just not there, and I've looked everywhere."

Laura started for Willow's room. Her first instinct was to check the closet. It didn't look disturbed. Her duffle lay on the floor, untouched. All the hangers were still filled. Bryce came behind her and opened the drawers. Full. Both of them glanced at each other.

"I'm not sure what is happening, but we need to look for her." Bryce glanced at Teddy. "Wake the house. We'll check the neighborhood, airport, bus station. Maybe she got spooked by our conversation."

"What if we found her out and—" Laura started.

Bryce shook his head. "No, we're not starting there. She is family. Until I know for sure she has burned us, we will assume she is on our side."

She nodded. Though she ran the team, he was still her husband. Many would be surprised how she honored that. It probably wasn't easy being married to such a strong woman. "Okay. Let's get everyone up. Bryce is right. We need to start a search."

****

After looking for Willow all night, Laura was only able to sleep for a few hours. Every fiber of her body desired more rest, but memories of being betrayed by so many people over the last few years plagued her. Finding Willow wasn't just about retrieving a family member, it was about protecting their position. What if Willow really was a spy and told someone where her team was? Could her absence mean trouble for them all? It almost always did. Laura would not lose another family member to S.I.U. or any other organization. If she had to kill one of her own to protect the rest of them, she would. But that, in and of itself, hurt her heart. She loved them all. Even if Willow betrayed them, she cared about her. S.I.U. had always discouraged relationships of any kind for that very reason. It often blinded people from doing what must be done.

Laura slid her second boot on and tied the laces. A yawn escaped just as Bryce exited the bathroom. He cupped both hands over his newly shaved head and sat on the edge of the bed. His half-mast eyelids and dark circles said he, too, was wiped out. He maybe slept an hour more than her, but that wasn't much.

"You okay?"

He nodded. "I'm just worried."

"That she's okay or that she's betraying us?"

He nodded again. "Yeah."

Laura reached in the side drawer by the bed and withdrew her gun. She checked the chamber and safety before shoving it into a shoulder holster. "We have to go back out. You ready?"

"Yeah, one second. I'll meet you in a moment." He grabbed his boots as she exited into the living room.

The smell of coffee lingered in the air. Teddy met her with a mug and a cranberry orange scone. "Good morning, our fearless leader. Did you get any sleep? I know the answer is no, and therefore, I have made homemade scones. Well, sort of homemade. They came in a box, and I added water. But still baked with love."

"Do you know how much I love you, Teddy? You are always my ray of sunshine in a very dark world."

A slight tint of red lined his cheeks. "Thanks."

"How did you end up so—" She paused, glancing at Deshawn, who sat at the table nursing a cup of coffee, before finishing her statement. "Happy."

"I come from a very dark background. I had to make a decision years ago. I figured I would learn to rise above it and not let it have me." He placed the plated scone and a cup of coffee on the counter and motioned for her to sit. "Two creams and one sweetener, the way you like it."

Laura smiled and slid onto the stool.

Helena entered yawning. "Something smells good."

"Teddy made scones."

"I love you, Teddy."

Another red-faced smile lit up his features. "If I knew I would get this much love, I might have made these months ago." He grabbed a spatula and plated another scone for Helena. "Coffee?"

"Yes, please. I hope it's strong. That was a long night." She rubbed hands over eyes and yawned again. "Myers is still gone. Are Charlie and Eri back yet?"

"I'm not sure. They said they'd keep looking, and we could take shifts." Laura lifted the light pastry to her mouth and nibbled a soft bite. "This is good."

"Where do you suppose she is?" Helena asked, as she reached for the creamer at the end of the counter.

"I wish I knew. I know she revealed something pretty significant last night, but I didn't think we were mean to her, were we?" Laura glanced at Teddy, as he knew Willow best and was also good at gauging situations when it came to emotions. Not something Laura had mastered.

"Um," he shrugged, "she seemed okay. I mean, she obviously knew it wasn't the best conversation, but didn't act like she would bolt."

"Where would she go?" Laura took a sip of her coffee. The dark aroma woke her senses. If only it could give her wisdom too.

Bryce entered and smiled. "Hey, Teddy, I will take whatever it is you're serving up."

"How'd you know?"

"Spidey senses."

Laura laughed. "What he means is a snout for sweet stuff. Teddy made—"

Charlie and Eri staggered in from outside. Their faces revealed the answer, even before she asked, "Any luck?"

Charlie pinched his lips together and glanced at Myers.

"She didn't leave, Laura." Myers held up a clump of red hair. "She was taken."

Chapter Three

Willow worked to open her eyes. They felt so heavy. Groggily, she peeked through her lids. *Where am I?* She couldn't see much. Some sort of material covered one eye, but the other one slightly peered around the edge. The room lay dark, but thanks to some light seeping through the cracks in the walls, she was able to make out several forms. From the smells and shapes, she guessed it to be a laundry room.

Clumps of material lay all around her and what looked to be a washing machine and dryer were to her right. The sweet smell of laundry detergent made up for a foul odor of mildew and rust. Above, the sounds of scuffling noises and the creaking of old floorboards, combined with the occasional muffled sounds of people talking, set the tone. From what she could tell, it seemed like two people were there.

How did I get here? The last thing she remembered was going to sleep on the couch, watching a movie with Teddy, Myers, and Helena. She squeezed her eyes tight and worked to still her breath. Her mentor, Laura, had taught her to always do a self-assessment of the situation.

The back of her neck stung a bit. Chances are they drugged her. Her ankles appeared to be secured by duct tape, and her wrists were bound behind a pole by some type of cuffs. She wiggled, seeing if either would give way. No such luck.

She tried to envision what different people from her team would do. Teddy would keep it lighthearted. Visions of him prattling on made her grin. Laura would say, "Survive. Fight back." That was all Laura knew how to do. That gave Willow a purpose, a sense of confidence. She aspired to be that great some day. Often, she had asked her mentor for lessons. Even though Willow was a full-fledged agent, something she had been afraid to tell Laura, she still had a lot to learn. Part of the reason she was locked up at S.I.U. was for making so many silly mistakes. This time, she couldn't afford to be stupid. Remembering her training and being fully aware could save her life.

Above, the scuffling moved across the floor, and then, a door opened at the top. A shaft of light marked some stairs. "Should I take her water?" a woman asked with a thick country accent. Something about it sounded off. Forced even.

"We want her alive, don't we?" a man replied with a matched southern charm. "Here, hurry and take this to her."

Willow closed her eyes and allowed herself to go limp.

The woman's footsteps rattled the steps, and then, she was by her side. "She's not awake yet."

"Well, wake her. We have to get going."

The woman yanked hard on the rag around Willow's face and shoved her head up. The outline indicated the woman wore a ski mask. That was good. Maybe their plan wasn't to kill her after all. If she couldn't identify her captors, there was always hope of being freed later on.

"Drink this." The woman put the bottle to Willow's lips. She drank as much as she could, most of it dribbling down her chin.

"Why am I here?" Willow asked, once the bottle was pulled away.

The woman didn't answer but clicked out a knife and cut the duct tape from Willow's ankles. She walked around the pole and unlocked the cuffs. Willow clenched her fist and was just about to punch, when she heard the sound of a shotgun being cocked at the top of the stairwell.

"Just in case you have any stupid ideas," the man said.

Willow nodded. She would wait.

"Let's go." The woman pushed her forward.

The steps had rot, creaking with every step. The outside light at the top of the stairs burned her eyes. The silhouette of a man with a rifle made her pause, but the woman nudged her up and out the door. Willow glanced around, confused. It looked like suburbia. The house was nicely decorated in contemporary blues and grays. Family pictures decorated the walls, several candles burned around the room, leaving a vanilla fragrance, and a beautiful ornate rug lay at her feet. *Where am I?*

The man adjusted her blindfold, and the room became dark. First, she heard what sounded like the pulling of duct tape, and then, she felt it being wound around her hands. A moment later, one of them pushed her down onto the couch that had been to her right and wound the tape around her ankles again.

"Is she secure?" the woman asked.

He touched the blindfold. "Yeah, good."

"Oh, it feels good to take that thing off," the woman said, and then, something soft hit Willow's arm. She assumed it must have been the ski mask.

The two began to speak in muffled whispers a few feet away. Willow exhaled slowly and tried to still her breathing, concentrating on their tones, hoping to understand by using all her senses. The country accents were now gone. "This will never work if they don't know we took her," the woman whispered. There was something familiar about her voice. "You know everything rides on that one idea."

"Trust me. I left a wad of her hair in the bush by the door. If they are as good as the boss, and you say they are, they'll find it. No problem."

"Are we ready when they get here?"

"Despite what I've told you, you still haven't told me why they would even come here? It doesn't mean anything."

The woman laughed and said in a regular tone, "Because I have left my own clues, my incompetent friend."

"Do not insult me. You know I'm a higher rank."

Rank? S.I.U.? Willow tried to sit up, though difficult without the use of her hands and feet.

"Are you sure we want to keep her in here and not in the basement?" he asked. "It seems more—"

"Trust me, you want her close until they are ready up there, just in case her people show up."

Somebody dropped down next to her. Wind whipped by her face. Likely, they were checking out if she could see. "It is pathetic really." The country accent had returned. "All this time, they have been running from S.I.U. Killing and locking up anyone who had any affiliation with the agency, and yet, two of the agent's operatives were right under their noses the entire time." The woman grabbed Willow's chin. "Isn't that right Agent Willow Briggs? A traitor to her oath and people."

Willow's heart rate increased. Somehow this woman knew her. And though she was trying to disguise her voice, Willow was sure she knew the woman, too. She just had to concentrate, to remember. It was always hard to discern things with a blindfold on. But the agency had taught her to focus in on key elements. She could do this. Figure it out. She just had to keep her talking. "What do you want from me?"

"In all honesty, I want you to die for my cause."

"And what cause is that?"

The woman stood and moved away from her. "For all of you to die. That is my cause. Pretty powerful, no?"

"All of whom?"

There was some whispering and a slight pause before she answered, "Your hypothetical family, of course."

"Did we wrong you in some way?"

The room grew quiet. Neither male nor female spoke. Did someone motion the other out? Had Willow pressed too much? She listened, hard. A slight creak could be heard a few yards away, and then, a door closed. Was she alone?

Assuming she might be, Willow leaned her head down to the side of the couch. What felt like a pillow scratched her cheek. She rubbed her head against it, trying to hook the blindfold. It took a few tries, but eventually, it worked, and the cloth fell down around her neck. The room was empty.

Willow peered around. What could she use? A burning candle sat to her left on a table. This would likely hurt, but she had to try. She scooted to the end of the couch, then hopped up on the end table and held her binding over the flame. Heat and then pain shot through wrists. She bore down, not wanting to scream, trying to block out the sting. The smell of burning hair and plastic wafted to her nose. It started to loosen. It was working. The door opened. Her eyes went wide. Willow snapped the wristband, ready to fight. She looked up and met her male captor's gaze. Her heart sank.

Chapter Four

Teddy paced behind the kitchen counter, not happy with any of the answers their crew had. Why weren't they doing something? Anything? All this speculation was making his head hurt. Usually, he was the one spreading optimism, but he didn't feel much joy right now. Whether anyone knew it or not, Willow meant something to him. They had been in this together from the moment of their rescue last year. They jokingly called themselves the odd men out. Not that they were ever treated that way, but it gave them a bond. Truth be told, for a while, he even had a crush on her. Kind of silly since she was completely out of his league and a few years older. But they were friends, and he wanted her back.

"We're wasting time!" Teddy slapped the counter.

Everyone stopped talking, eyes wide, and stared his way, obviously not used to that behavior coming from him.

Eri touched his hand. "I know it feels that way, but we don't know where she is, and until we do—"

"I've got something." Charlie looked up from his laptop. The group huddled around to see the screen. In front of them was a satellite map. He fingered a set of roads. "I have the vehicle driving west on Pepper Lane, turning right here on Amistad, and then going left in this neighborhood just past Orange."

"You're sure?"

Charlie nodded.

"Okay then. Everyone load up." Laura grabbed a rifle bag from the counter. "We don't know how long they'll be there."

The team didn't need to be told again. Each grabbed his or her various gear. The sound of loading guns reverberated around the house. Within minutes, they were climbing in the back of their black van. Adrenaline coursed through Teddy's veins. It had been a while since he had been in the field. The last time had been when they took out S.I.U. almost eight months ago. Though he was proficient with a gun, he was rusty with hand-to-hand combat. Many times, Laura had encouraged him to practice his skills, but he just wanted to forget the old life and move on to this one.

Taking a job at a local movie theater surprised everyone, but he'd rather clean up popcorn than shoot someone. The rest of the team had been on various missions to rescue S.I.U. agents and trafficked teens, but he opted to stay back. He wanted to forget all of it. To move on. Feel like a normal teenager. But apparently, Laura had been right all along; this life would never leave them alone. Teddy sighed. They would always be fighting. Normal was just a figment of delusion created by some sit-com.

"Slow down." Laura leaned forward in the passenger seat and pointed through the front window to a two-story white house on the right side of the street. "Look, that's a vehicle like ours. That is probably it."

Charlie decelerated to a stop along the curb and then shut off the engine. "How do we want to play this?"

Laura looked in the rearview mirror to see Deshawn had pulled over as well and touched her com. "Come on up."

Once everyone was together behind the vehicle, Charlie asked again, "So how do we want to play this?"

"Charlie, you stay here ready to drive, listening on coms, and tracking the area via satellite." Laura glanced at Bryce. "You and Teddy take the back. Eri, you find a way to the second floor. Helena, you keep a watch out. Myers and I will go through the front on my count. Questions?"

"How do we know she's in there?" Myers asked.

Laura glanced down the street and sighed. "Because, that isn't a van like ours. That *is* our van."

****

The air was silent for the exception of rustling leaves and the squeaking of a swing in the backyard. Teddy knelt by the screen door in the back of the house. This hardly seemed like a place for this—in the heart of suburbia. The slight smell of cut grass tickled his nose. Willing himself not to sneeze, he leaned his face on the side of his arm.

"You okay?" Bryce asked.

"Allergic to the grass."

Bryce shook his head, basically saying, "Don't sneeze, man."

Mind over matter. Teddy had this. And then he didn't. Without warning, air shot from his nose and mouth.

Bryce snapped in the com. "Now!"

Everyone swept into action, and the night became sounds of boots pushing in doors, broken glass, gunshots, and smoke.

"Clear," Laura yelled from the front.

"Clear," Bryce said from the kitchen.

Eri's voice didn't come. "Eri," Charlie said over the com.

Nothing.

"Eri," he said again.

Bryce pointed two fingers at his eyes, then pointed one up and nodded, before creeping forward.

Teddy understood. They were going upstairs. With guns ready, they crept outside the door and to a wooden staircase to the left of the kitchen. Bryce kept his back to the wall, and Teddy swung his gun to the end to stairs. In unison, they inched up to the top. A faint whimpering noise came from last room.

"Upstairs," Bryce whispered in the com.

"Got it," Laura said back.

One guard stood at the door.

Bryce glanced at the staircase. Laura's head popped up. She steadied her gun on the railing and nodded. Myers passed her and shifted around the corner to stand between Bryce and Teddy.

He shot a dart into the side of a guard's neck. The man crumpled to the floor.

Laura motioned for Teddy to take care of the body.

Teddy closed his eyes and inhaled. His heart beat like a jackrabbit on sugar. *It has been too long.* Could he still do this? He complied and dragged the body down the hall and out of the way.

When he came back, he spotted Bryce holding up one finger, slowly raising another. When his third one lifted, Myers kicked the door in. The three men rushed the room and then stopped. Willow sat in a metal chair in the center, blindfolded, gagged, and surrounded by a dozen or more red laser dots.

Nausea swept through Teddy's core. *Focus.* He glanced around, wondering the source of the red dots. A slew of holes covered the walls, which likely held guns or claymore mines. What did they do?

"Willow, we're here, but you need to keep still, okay?" Bryce said, glancing around at the situation.

She moaned but didn't move.

Bryce backed out of the room, probably to go get Laura.

"What's going on?" Charlie asked over the com. "Any word on Eri?"

Myers and Teddy exchanged glances. Did they tell him? "Eri's not here, man," Myers whispered. "But we found Willow. We need you to bring your laptop."

"What do you mean Eri's not there?"

"We'll explain when you get up here. But get up here, now!" Myers dropped a load of expletives, which he always seemed to do to emphasize his point. Hopefully, he wouldn't start punching things.

Laura entered and knelt down. With the confidence Teddy always admired, she peered from every angle. She rose and peeked at the side of one of the holes. "Could be claymore mines, not sure. Deshawn will know more. But one thing I am sure of, if we cross any of those beams, she's toast."

"We can't leave her like that," Teddy said.

"We won't, but we have to think this through." Laura pulled out a cell phone and dialed. Placing it to her ear, she said, "Yeah, hi, it's Laura. It's time."

Chapter Five

Willow sat in the chair, trying not to move. Trying not to scream. There was no clue available to determine her situation. Only assumption. Something was in her ears, over her eyes, and in her mouth. Voices echoed all around her, but she could not discern their words. The loss of senses gave the illusion of being buried alive— one of her biggest fears. It could not beat her.

Instead, she would focus on other things. Like, how long had she been like this? What could be happening? It had to be a bomb. For that reason alone, she would be still. One wrong movement and that could be it. Though she had hated her time at S.I.U., she was thankful now for every moment in the pit. Harding had often made the team stay overnight in an underground tunnel filled with insects and other creatures. The point was to help with claustrophobia and to learn to blank out pain. Coming out always took a week or two of medical treatment, but it got easier. Today, it helped.

Though exhausted, sleep was beyond her. Fear was enough, but it was not everything. Her back muscles burned, her neck ached, and her feet tingled and were numb. *Inhale through the nose. Exhale into the rag. Inhale through the nose. Exhale into the rag.* Once again, she tried to focus on her heartbeat and not her situation. It was not enough. Anxiety rose in her chest.

What else could she think about to distract herself? Maybe she could pray. Maybe Harding wasn't the only one to prepare her for today. Growing up in church may also have prepared her. At the time, she only went to church to get away from her angry alcoholic father. When the church bus started stopping on her street, Willow took it.

It was nice to see all those happy people. And the donuts and candy weren't bad either. But what had she learned those days that might help right now? There was a Psalm she liked. Was it twenty-three or four? *Something about overcoming evil...* What were the words? She couldn't remember all them, but what she could remember instantly gave her peace. She cited them in her head and tried to repeat them in a whisper. It helped some until the room grew uncomfortable—stifling hot.

Sweat began to bead on her brow and dripped down her back and face. *Inhale, exhale. Slow your breathing.*

Something was wrong. Loud thunderous sounds echoed in her ears. Stars began to form before her eyes, and she thought she might pass out. Memories flooded her mind. Was this the flash before she died? No, it was the reality that this all was happening because of one decision so long ago. One moment in time. It only took a few seconds to completely change the course of her life.

It still played clear in her thoughts. July Fourth—a national holiday—supposed to be a day to celebrate. Her dad was drunker that usual. For some dumb reason, he decided Willow needed to stay close to home that night—something about there being too much partying and too many drunk drivers out there. Not that being home with an abusive alcoholic father was much safer. But he dictated, and she obeyed, per usual.

Right after sunset, he began to have one his tirades. Being yelled at and demeaned, Willow retreated to her room and locked it with a chair. It didn't take but a moment for him to react. He stumbled outside her door and started banging and cursing. Fear clutched her throat, and sobs wracked her body. For a moment, she folded to the ground and allowed it to have her. Then something happened. Boldness, a desire to fight like never before, sent a thought that would change everything, one she probably should have ignored.

"Dad, if you calm down, I'll make you dinner."

The knocking stopped. He let out a few choice words, and then, his footsteps retreated down the hall, followed by the sound of the TV being turned on.

Willow slipped into the hall and peered over to her father on the couch. *Occupied.* It was her only chance. She ran for the stairs and down them into the basement. Flicking on the light, she quickly glanced around for any kind of weapon. Her gaze caught anti-freeze. The memory of some woman killing her family with anti-freeze occurred to her, but then she dismissed it. That would take entirely too long. Her eye caught sight of an axe that sat against the side of a workbench. Could she do this? Kill her own father? But she had to, didn't she? There was no other way out. It was the only way she would ever be free.

She lifted it with both hands. It was heavier than she anticipated. A quick swing determined it was not *too* heavy. Her heart thundered in her chest, and her breathing labored. Stars fluttered through her vision.

Don't black out.

At the top of the stairs, she could hear some military movie playing in the background. Something he always watched. She peeked out. His head lay against the back of the sofa. She moved toward him. Squeezing her eyes closed, she tried to find a place in her core to do this, but it only screamed "no." She proceeded to lower the axe. No way could she take his life. It wasn't in her to murder someone, especially her dad.

"I brought beer." The screen door opened, revealing Mrs. Tyler from next door. The widow often came over to spoon with her dad, despite their obvious age difference. Her wrinkled mouth dropped as she looked from the axe to Willow to the man on the couch. She backed up, stuttering, while pulling out her cell phone.

Her father pivoted around. His eyes went wide, then fierce. He leapt over the couch in one leap. Willow ran for her room again, axe still in hand.

"Come here, you little—!"

She slammed the door before the curses fell.

The door pushed open.

She leaned against it, pushing it back.

His hand came through the crack. She swung the axe, slicing a knuckle. He pulled back with a yelp; she slammed the door and then pushed the chair under the handle. She inched back and folded to the ground, still clutching the weapon in her hands, silently praying for help. Tears burned her cheeks. It seemed like seconds later, sirens sounded in the street. Red and blue lights flickered through the open blinds and around her room.

A new knock pounded on the door. "This is the

police. Open up!"

Willow placed the axe on the bed and crossed to the door. "Show me a badge under the door, and I'll open it."

"Lady, do you see the lights? Open the door, or we'll kick it in."

Willow steeled herself for anything. With trembling hands, she moved the chair. The door popped open, and two tall men in uniform stood there brandishing weapons pointed at her head.

"On your knees, now!" one commanded.

She dropped, no longer afraid. It had to be bad when being locked up by the police felt better than being at home. They drug her out and into the back of a car. At the station, they took her statement and assured her she would be freed. Maybe she would have been, but Greenstone came for her. He said she was lost and needed a family. The story he spun said he would provide her a new way to live. A better way. Later, the truth would come out. The fact she could kill her own father seemed to put her on the S.I.U. radar. Little did they know she wasn't strong enough to do it; that given time, she would have put the axe down and made him dinner.

A sharp pain shot up Willow's back, bringing her back to the present situation. All memory returned to being stuck in a hard metal chair, ready to die. Her whole life seemed to revolve around bad circumstances. Only for a short time in her entire life had she felt any sense of happiness. Her new family—Laura and her husband, Bryce—had taken her in, with no questions and no suspicions. Not once had they asked why she came to S.I.U. in the first place. The entire thing with them seemed surreal. *Too happy.* Of course, it couldn't last. No bliss ever did.

Though she hated to admit defeat, today she felt vanquished. Soon the bomb would take her life. What happened next, she didn't know. Her heart would miss her dear friends Teddy and Helena. She had become such great friends with both. That hurt worse than the idea of death. At least in death, there wasn't any pain. Joining God would at last be the freedom she always sought. Maybe even joy. But not for those who would mourn her. Teddy would take it the worst. His tender heart always made her smile. Today, it made her sad. Fresh tears seeped into the rag around her eyes.

Truthfully, she didn't really know what would happen after the bomb took her. Visions of Sunday school skits and Bible stories came back to her memory. She focused on that and the thoughts of heaven. Whatever it took, she needed to get ready.

Chapter Six

Laura discontinued the call. This was bigger than her training; Deshawn knew a lot about this kind of thing. They were still getting to know him, but from what she had seen, he was a genius with all things tactical. Before being caught, his job in the military had been to clear areas with bombs and snipers. He was a big guy, and few would mess with him. His stature even made the mighty Myers look diminutive.

Deshawn and Charlie appeared above the stairs at the same time. Charlie ducked in a far room and returned with a chair. He placed it in the hallway, sat, and opened his computer on his lap. "If you want me fully functional here, I need you to tell me…" His eyes met hers. "Where is Eri?"

"I totally get it. We all do." Laura crossed the hallway to touch his shoulder. "My best guess, Charlie, is they took her when we first arrived. We can't really know for sure until we get Willow out of here. Time is of the essence. Can you focus? Or should I get Myers to do it instead?"

"Tell me what we have."

Laura knew that would work. Myers and Charlie had a healthy competition about who was the better hacker. Charlie probably was, but Myers was a close second. She looked up. "Deshawn."

The black man nodded and ducked into the room.

Laura followed.

He trailed the course of the beams with his eyes, looking from the holes in the wall to the chair. He knelt down and studied the ground near her feet. "Good news or bad?"

"Both."

"Good news, no pressure plate."

Laura crossed her arms and faced him. "And the bad?"

"If we move her, every mine will be triggered and people will die."

Now what? Laura paced out the door and down the hall. She stopped in front of Charlie. "Any technical options?"

"I was hoping it would be triggered by some sort of device, but they went old school. Nothing I can do here."

Tears welled in Laura's eyes. Not something that happened often. But how did they save their friend? It seemed impossible.

"I have an idea," Teddy said.

"What?" Laura said a bit sharply, and Teddy jumped back. "Sorry."

Teddy shrugged. "It's okay. We're all tense. I'd probably yell at me, too, if I weren't me." He smiled and then continued, "This may sound silly..." He glanced at each of them. "But you know the old Bugs Bunny cartoons where they saw a hole in the ceiling and the person drops through. Do you think that is possible? Crazy, right? Could it work? It would be really cool if it could work."

They all stared at him. It did sound ridiculous.

Laura pondered that thought. Would it work? Or would it get them all killed?

"This is a tall house," Bryce said. "How do we saw a hole?"

"Not to mention there is probably more than a simple floorboard between—" Laura started to say, but then stopped. "But wait, what if we were able to get her from above somehow?"

Bryce titled his head sideways. "I don't understand."

Laura walked back to the doorway and pointed. "All the beams are at her chest and back. Could we go in the attic and lower something down?"

"She'd still get hit the minute the beams are broken," Deshawn said.

"Dang!" Laura began to pace.

"Come on. Stay with us." Bryce slid a hand to the middle of her back. "We'll figure something out."

Willow mumbled through the cloth.

Laura tried to listen. "What is she saying?"

"I think she may be citing something."

Charlie ripped the beanie off his head, revealing a mop of hair. The pain in his eyes said this was not his top mission. They needed to hurry.

"Is there a way to disable the claymores without crossing the beams?" Bryce pointed to the holes.

Deshawn held up a finger and walked back in the room. A moment later, he exited and nodded. "If we can access them through the other side of the wall, it is possible. But any disturbance to the mines, and they will likely go off."

"So old school here too. No electric saws," Laura said.

"No, that wouldn't work either." Charlie stood and snapped his laptop closed. "I say we go purely new. We use lasers to cut the back of the walls."

****

It took hours, and Laura felt bad for Charlie. Without knowing Eri's whereabouts, he was not doing well. Each second that went by changed his demeanor. One minute, he was crying; the next, he was angry and kicking the wall. If they didn't do something soon, the cork would pop, and he would do something irrational.

Laura stepped over a mound of sheetrock and leaned next to where Charlie was scooping out some wall. "Charlie, I think you should take Helena and do some recon work on where Eri might have gone. Tap into satellites or whatever it is that you do. When you find something, come get one of us."

Clear relief washed over his face. "Thanks."

She nodded as the two left down the stairs.

"Smart move. He wasn't going to last much longer," Bryce said, setting down a laser and peeling back drywall.

"I began to worry that any moment he might have just busted in there and ripped Willow out of the chair." Laura glanced down the hall at the various holes that were now exposed from the hallway. "Now what?"

"We disconnect them one by one. Deshawn taught me how. Let me show you." Bryce pointed to the wires and the laser connection. It only took a second, and the first laser dropped off.

Each of them walked to other openings and did the same. Laura went to the one in the far bedroom to check out one of the holes Charlie had created. Leaning down, something caught the corner of her vision on the far nightstand. An ivory-colored envelope with the word *BLACK* scribbled in felt pen.

Her heart accelerated. She stepped around the bed and snatched it up. Probably a stupid motion, as there could have been a booby trap or toxin. Did she open it? What if it held a contaminant inside? "Guys…"

Bryce and Myers ran in and glanced at her shaking hand. Deshawn entered right behind them. Teddy came in last and peeked through. "What is that?"

"A message from Willow's captors, I presume." Laura stretched her hand out so they could see it better.

"Addressed to you?" Bryce reached for it, but Laura pulled back.

"We don't know if it is safe. I probably shouldn't have grabbed it myself."

Worry showed on Bryce's face.

"You have gloves on. Here." Teddy handed her a dust mask he had found in the basement. "I was using it to keep the plaster out of my mouth. I have allergies. You can use it to protect yourself."

Laura could have kissed him. He always surprised her. "Thanks." She pulled the mask over her face and adjusted the elastic back. "Everyone move back."

Once they had stepped into the hallway, she slid her finger through the seal on the envelope and withdrew its contents. Inside was a single lined piece of paper which read, "We've only just begun."

Chapter Seven

Teddy chewed his nails, waiting anxiously until the last laser disappeared and Deshawn yelled, "Clear." The minute it came, he ran to Willow's side.

"Wait," Laura yelled, but it was too late.

He dropped the cloth from Willow's eyes and mouth. Her smile said it all. He hugged her tight, every pore melting with relief. "I'm so glad you're okay."

"My ears. I can't hear."

Teddy pulled the plugs from her ears and then walked around to the back to cut the ties from her hands and feet. The rest stopped packing up the claymores and met her with big grins.

Willow tried to stand, but her legs seemed to buckle. Teddy caught her and carried her out of the room to the bed in the other room.

"We should get her to a hospital," Teddy said.

Laura shook her head. "Not safe."

Of course, Laura would say no. Teddy frowned. *Always afraid of those in the shadows.*

"We will call our friend, Dr. Craig," Laura pulled out her cell. "He still owes us for helping his sister."

Willow tried to stand again.

"Shouldn't you rest first?" Teddy reached out to her. "After all, trauma does more to the body than we think. It can affect our mind, body, and soul. It initiates permanent alterations in the ventromedial prefrontal cortex of the brain and can cause serious emotional scars to the amygdala that will most certainly—"

Willow held up a hand and offered a closed-mouth grin. "I'm okay. I actually need to walk around and get circulation back in my legs." She slid to the corner of the bed. "Not to mention, I'm starving."

"Let's get her home, and we can make her something to eat." Laura motioned for Myers to help her walk.

The two guys wrapped her arms around their necks and lifted her up. Sweat beaded on her lip, as she was obviously working hard to walk on rubbery legs. Teddy couldn't help feeling sorry for her. There was an empathy that always got in the way of his being any sort of good agent. He'd only been with the agency a few months when he saw the inside of their prison cell for the first time.

Skills were no problem. He could kick butt and shoot a gun better than most. It was his heart and conscience that always deterred him. The S.I.U. organization was a cold, calculated machine with absolutely no compassion, or patience for those who had any.

Teddy was all heart. In another life, he would likely have ended up a medical doctor, pastor, or social worker. S.I.U. only kidnapped him because he was living on the street due to his parental issues. Most of those on this team were ex-cons, but not him. He was just in the wrong place at the wrong time.

Once they got to the edge of stairs, Laura stopped them. "Someone get a hold of Charlie and find out where we are with finding Eri."

"Is he still outside?" Myers asked.

"If he's not, we can take our other van. I saw the keys on a hook in the entryway."

The group ascended the staircase and shuffled to the door.

"I'll call." Bryce touched the screen of his cell phone. "Hey, man. Where are we on—? Sure. Yeah, one minute. Okay. Sounds good."

"So?" Laura asked, opening the passenger door for Teddy to help Willow get in.

"Charlie found something, but he needs some of us to go with him," Bryce said.

She nodded. "Teddy, why don't you drive Willow home? The doctor should be by some time tonight. Deshawn, Myers, Bryce, and I will follow Charlie. We are still missing one of our own, so this day is not over yet."

"Okay." Teddy took the keys from Bryce and walked around to the driver's seat. "How do I get a hold of the good doctor, if I need to?"

"His number is on the fridge." Laura waved, and the rest joined Charlie and Helena at the other van.

Teddy walked around to the driver's side. He was glad to stay with Willow. His body felt drained. Going on another mission didn't seem physically possible. Besides, his worry was more attached with his good friend, Willow. He loved Eri, but he was more connected to Willow. The pain Charlie was feeling, Teddy had already experienced today. He started the engine and pulled out into the street. "How about we get a quick bite at that chicken and biscuit place down the street instead of eating at home?"

"You know me so well." She squeezed his hand.

"But maybe go through the drive-thru. I'm not up for going in right now."

"Of course."

They drove in silence until they reached the yellow and blue building. He pulled the car up to the sign and ordered a bucket of chicken and a box of biscuits. "Can I get extra strawberry jam and butter?"

"And honey," Willow said.

"And honey."

The cashier read back their order. "Pull around to the second window, and we'll have your order ready for you."

"Thank you."

"My pleasure."

Willow visibly cringed.

"You okay?"

"For some reason, I hate that expression. All the fast food places say it, which makes it just seem insincere."

"I like it."

She smiled. "You would."

They got their order and endured one more "My pleasure," before they were on their way.

****

Across the room, Willow chewed her food almost methodically, staring at the blank TV.

His heart ached for her. Teddy wiped his hand on a napkin and slid over toward her on the couch. "Are you okay?"

"What?" She blinked and turned to look at him.

"Are you okay?"

She nodded, offering him a soft smile. "It's just a lot to process. I thought I would die only a few hours ago."

"I thought so, too." He placed his plate onto the coffee table and turned to her. "I don't know what I would have done if anything had happened to you."

She set her plate next to his and bent her knee up on the couch, so she faced him. "This life of ours…" Tears formed in her eyes. "My fear is it doesn't get much better than this, you know? That this is it for us." She let out an anguished sigh, her voice thick with emotion, as a tear slid down her cheek. "But I can't live like this forever. Always looking over our shoulders. Always afraid. Never happy."

Teddy took her hand in his and offered a consoling smile. If this event proved anything, it validated that he loved her, though he expected little in return. "Are you really unhappy?"

She shrugged. "There are moments, I suppose, when I feel like if I don't breathe, it might stay good."

He smiled. "For me, too."

An uncomfortable silence fell between them which rarely happened, because Teddy always had something to say. He licked his lips. "I think this is a different enemy."

"How so?"

Teddy shrugged. "It just seemed unlike the attacks from before."

"I know S.I.U. is involved somehow, but I agree, something is different." She withdrew her hand, wiped her face, and stood, pacing. "The two people with me were skilled, but not emotionless. I think this is retribution, not tactical." She faced Teddy. "I saw one of them. I recognized him but couldn't place him. I would guess S.I.U. is where I know him, but I don't know." She paced a bit more, then added, "What if it is S.I.U., but not a sanctioned hit? It felt more like someone we made very angry, and they are making us pay." A red dot appeared on Willow's forehead.

Teddy leapt and tackled her to the floor. Glass rained over them as shots hit the wall. Shards of glass sliced his back. He screamed in pain, but quickly, worked to block it out. No time to be a victim. He scrambled to his knees, helped Willow to do the same, and pushed her to the hall. "Move!"

The two of them shimmed on haunches as bullets rained overhead. They reached the door that opened to the cellar. It has been Laura's plan in case they were ever attacked. Once inside, Teddy bolted the door and flipped on the light switch. The room had been reinforced with steel and supplies. They would be safe here.

"You're bleeding," Willow said.

"We'll deal with that in a moment. There's a first aid kit on the left." He scrambled to the bottom of stairs and flipped on the laptop. "Right now, I need to let the team know we're under attack."

Chapter Eight

Laura's heart dropped as she slipped her phone back into her pocket. "Our base is under attack."

Bryce glanced at her from the driver's seat. "What?"

"I just got the 9-1-1 alert from Teddy. Someone is shooting at them. We have to go home now."

Myers sat forward in the van. "Hey, I just got an alert from Teddy. The house is under attack."

Laura nodded. "Yeah, we got it too."

"What do we do?" Bryce asked.

Charlie sat in the other van on his laptop, pouring through street videos, hoping to get a hit on their assailant's direction. Right now, they didn't know anything. But if their house was under attack, that may actually be a clue.

"We need to go home." Laura jumped out of the van, walked up the passenger side door, and rapped on the window.

The glass lowered, and Charlie glanced her way. "What's up? Did you find her? I haven't found—"

"No, the house is under attack. We have to go back."

His face fell. "But I can't leave her."

Laura folded her arms on the sill of the window. "Chances are these are the same people, Charlie. If we can capture one, they can lead us to her. You know this camera thing is not helping. They are smart. They didn't even take our van. They had some other way of escape and covered their tracks. Right now, we have some of our people in danger."

He peeked out through messy strands of hair, his expression unclear.

"Charlie?"

Slowly, he nodded.

Laura turned to the other van with thumbs up and then ran around to jump into the passenger's seat. "We need to hurry."

"The bunker should hold, right?" Bryce asked, pulling out in the street.

"Yeah, sure it will, unless they decided to blow it up."

****

Smoke was visible from the end of the street. Laura's stomach turned sour. Were they too late? Had the bad guys set the house on fire? Could Laura and her team just have spent the entire day saving one of their own, just to lose two of them instead? It hurt her soul to even think about it. She pointed to the curb. "Stop here."

Charlie pulled over to the side of the road and cut the engine and lights. The other van did the same. The sun barely peeked over the horizon, but it still wasn't dark enough to block their approach. This group, whomever they were, was good. Laura's team had to be smarter than them.

"Let's go join them in the other van to figure this out." Laura bounded to the sidewalk and met him at the back. "Are there any supplies in this van?"

He shook his head. "Only my laptop."

Likely, the bad guys had cleaned it out. It is what she would do. "Okay." Together, they walked to the side door and joined Deshawn, Myers, Helena, and Bryce.

"Is our house on fire?" Helena asked with a stunned expression.

"I don't know. It's possible." Laura prayed it wasn't. With all that metal, the basement could be like an actual oven. "We need to hurry, just in case."

"Laura, why don't you and I go around on the canyon side?" Bryce pointed to the overhang that sat just below their property. It was one of the reasons they chose it. One jump with a cord and they could be in a different part of the city. "We can sneak in from the back without being detected."

"Good idea. Charlie, you monitor from here. The rest of you take the front." Laura opened a large case filled with various weapons and began handing them out. "I suggest masks and vests."

Everyone prepared, and within a few minutes, they were running to their appointed destinations. Laura dropped down into a clump of bushes, just on the edge of the canyon, and maneuvered forward, hoping not to plummet to her death. Luckily, no one seemed to be outside. Were they in the house? There didn't appear to be any sort of vehicle either. But if they were smart, they would have parked farther down the block.

The smell of smoke lingered in the air, but it didn't smell like burning wood. It was more like a smoke grenade. Laura shimmied to the back window facing the kitchen and peered inside. Empty. Bryce tapped her shoulder and motioned with a nod and a point that he was going in the back door.

She nodded, keeping her gun pointed at the room, in case anyone appeared.

He unlocked the handle carefully and quietly, then pushed it just enough for him to squeeze through. Laura watched from behind. Inching forward, he glanced around, before waving for her to join him.

Shouts sounded from inside. The actual words were lost, but it sounded like Deshawn and Myers. Bryce ran from the kitchen in their direction. Laura ran inside to follow. All of them stood in the middle of the living room, pointing their guns at a figure with a hood. Deshawn ripped the hood off.

"Eri?"

"Did you say Eri?" Charlie said over the com.

"Yeah, Charlie, she's here," Bryce answered.

"What's going on?" Laura demanded pacing. None of this made sense. Why were they taking her people and giving them back. What was their play here? What could this game possibly solve?

Eri shook her head. "I have no idea how I got here. I remember someone at the other house grabbed me, and then I passed out. When I woke up, I smelled smoke and this hood was over my head. It's only been a few minutes."

Bryce punched in the code on the basement door and leaned in. "Teddy and Willow? You guys down there? The coast is clear."

A moment later, the two joined them on the landing. The back of Teddy's shirt was covered in blood, and Willow stood behind him holding the wound with what looked like an old blanket.

"Are you shot?" Laura asked.

He shook his head and dipped his head to the living room. "Glass."

Gazes followed his eyes to the busted living room window.

"I tried to patch it up, but they are too deep," Willow said.

"Go sit at the counter, Charlie. I'll get the mend kit." Helena walked to the back of the house.

"Go with her," Laura said to Deshawn. "We've had enough people disappearing on us today."

Deshawn dipped his head in agreement and followed her out.

"You're okay." Charlie wrapped Eri in his arms and squeezed. The two of them cried for a moment, before he said to Laura over Eri's shoulder, "We can't stay here anymore. They know we're here."

"Agreed. Let's get Teddy and Willow patched up and collect anything important. Twenty minutes top."

Helena returned with a small white metal box.

Myers started cursing. He spun around and punched a wall. Not that anyone was a surprised. "Just once, I thought that this might be it. You know?"

"We know," Laura sighed. If anyone knew, it was her. She had been leading this group of misfits from home to home for way too long. It was bound to wear on them all after a while. She was surprised Myers only tossed a few cuss words and fist. Right now, how she felt, she could easily do more.

Helena set the case down on the counter, then wrapped her arm around Myers' waist and whispered in his ear. His body visibly relaxed. He then moved to the basement door. "I'll go box up the supplies below."

Laura laughed as he disappeared. Things never

changed, but Helena was a godsend. Before her, no one could calm him down. "Sounds good. Let's go everyone."

"Don't we want to figure out who did this first?" Helena asked, as she pulled thread, bandages, and ointment from the box. "Or even ask why?"

"Of course. Just not here." Laura walked away to her bedroom. All of her being felt the same emotion Myers exhibited; she just had the ability to bottle it better. The thought of moving again not only angered her but also mentally hurt. All she wanted was to be left alone to live their lives like ordinary people. Laura had wanted to stay out of S.I.U.'s way, but her team had different ideas. They felt that, if there were kidnapped kids out there, they needed to rescue them.

That had become their mission many times over the last eight months. But mostly, it was sex-trafficked teens. Very rarely had they found pockets of S.I.U.'s kids. In her mind, if there were still agents operating, then this war was too big to fight. She had decided to no longer put her family in danger. But somehow, the danger found them anyway. They couldn't escape it. This was their destiny.

Chapter Nine

Willow stared out the window of the van, blinking repeatedly to keep more tears from falling. This whole experience had been too much. The replaying of her father's abuse came back full force. So many painful memories rolled around in her head. She wasn't sure what did more damage—being kidnapped, getting shot at, or taking the trek down her painful past.

"Are you okay?" Teddy whispered.

My constant caretaker. She didn't know how she would have made it this far without him by her side. Often, she had imagined them as becoming more than friends, but then she always pushed that thought away. She determined that having a relationship was a sure-fire way to mess up a friendship. Then she saw it happen. Helena's younger sister, Alicia seemed to have feelings for Teddy. And from what Willow determined, it was reciprocated. But just when something started to happen between them, it abruptly ended, and she took off. Teddy was devastated. He apologized like a million times, assuming everyone blamed him for her leaving. Of course, no one did. Alicia missed her home. Who could fault her for that? But to leave him behind? That could not happen to Willow and Teddy. He kept her grounded. Losing him would be a fatal blow to her psyche.

"Willow?" He touched her elbow.

"I'm fine." She shot him a tight grin over her shoulder in a vain effort to reassure him and then went back to watching the changing landscape. She could feel his stare on the back of her head. Attempting to block it out, she focused on what lay before her. On her right, lush trees stood with streams of light breaking through, and to her left, miles of canyon overlooked vast forests—so beautiful, but far from how she felt.

The mountains slowly turned into desert. Day started to become night. A gorgeous orange hue slipped above the vast, parched landscape. Willow yawned, having watched the transition like a show on TV. It had to have been more than eight hours before Charlie finally pulled off on an exit ramp and into a gas station. Everyone, obviously anxious to debark, scrambled from the van.

Willow joined them. Every muscle in her body screamed. Without warning, thunder cracked in the distance, and in an instant, rain and flashes of lightning joined it.

The group ran under an awning at the entrance of a mini-mart, laughing.

"Nice." Myers waved his hand over the water on his face. "I love a good summer shower."

"You're just mad because your hair got wet," Helena teased.

With apparent disregard for her sass, Myers asked the group, "Hey, are we grabbing food here?"

"If you want to, we can. Or we can find a fast food place close by." Laura laced her fingers with Bryce's. "Either way, I think we should find a place to stay for the night. I think we are getting a little loopy and need some serious rest."

"I saw a burger place up the road," Teddy said. "It's nothing fancy, but when I'm starved…a burger is a burger is a burger, am I right?" He elbowed Willow and winked. "Am I right?"

"Sure, Teddy, if you say so." Willow winked. He knew she didn't eat meat. Not because of any notion about animals being equal to humans, but just because with all the abuse to her body over the years, she chose to do better by it. Also, it drove Teddy crazy, which would be reason enough.

A few of them chuckled. One of Teddy's charms was bringing laughter to the group. It may not always be welcome, but it was usually needed.

"Okay, get any snacks you want, but we'll plan to grab burgers and find a motel." A bell rang at the top as Laura entered the store. "Ten minutes."

Willow followed, not sure what she would find. The air conditioning sent a chill on her wet skin. The light had an eerie green tint, and the shelves were filled with every man-made, chemically-altered food on the planet. This team loved their Styrofoam cheddar snacks and chemically enhanced beverages. Not Willow. She was the resident hippie who, besides only eating plants, also chose to only eat things that were created by God and nature. Of course, people like Teddy and Charlie loved to tease her whenever possible, calling her a rabbit or flower child. If it meant she lived longer and didn't get sick, so be it. Call her whatever they want. She stayed thin and healthy.

"So, Willow, what oats and hay substitute will you find in this assortment of divine goodness to satisfy your abnormal appetite?" Charlie held up a bag of artificially orange-colored something with a huge grin.

"Nothing on earth should be that color."

Teddy laughed. "Yes, which is probably why it is so sick."

"Sick is right." She weaved through the aisles, glancing at candy, cookies, chips, gum, mints, muffins—all of it processed and unappetizing. Finally, she spotted some organic popcorn, assorted nuts, and a package of dried apricots. That would have to do. They paid for their bounty and made their way back to the SUV.

Beautiful flashes of purple and white ignited against the darkening horizon. Unfortunately, the rain continued to downpour. The storm did little to cool everything off as the air felt muggy and thick, making it difficult to breathe.

Willow got in back and watched as Laura climbed in the passenger seat next to Bryce, who was now driving. "So, I asked the clerk if there were any motels close to here." She set a plastic bag at her feet and swung the door closed. "He said about five or so miles down the interstate we should spot a few. He also said there was a row of fast food chain restaurants next to it, so we can forgo the mystery burger joint and eat something we all recognize. Sorry, Teddy."

Teddy pretended to be offended, then grinned.

Within minutes, the vehicle pulled into a lane at a drive-thru. Everyone leaned over Bryce one by one to share his or her order to the talking box. Hungry-boy Teddy ordered two double cheeseburgers, an extra-large fry, an order of chicken strips with barbeque sauce, and a chocolate chip shake. Willow modestly ordered a garden salad with low-fat Italian dressing and an unsweetened iced tea.

Once they paid, Bryce drove them to a motel just alongside the freeway. Everyone's expressions looked tired and worn. It had been an exhausting twenty-four hours. No one talked as they ate, and once they were done, each returned to their room. Willow barely ate. She tossed the still full container and showered. The hot water relaxed her. Her eyes were heavy, but so was her mind.

She stretched out next to Helena. Within seconds, her roommate breathed in a steady rhythm. Though Willow's body needed it, her brain would not allow sleep. All of her day came back in dramatic flashes. Bad memories. Horrible thoughts. She folded the pillow behind her and readjusted herself.

Their current situation started to plague her thoughts. Where was her team going? Were they just running to run? Myers once said Laura often did that. She operated without a plan—no destination. How could they really disappear? Was the enemy following them? And who was the enemy? Was it S.I.U., or was this some other enemy? After all, her team had been freeing women in the sex trade, too. It was only a matter of time before one of those bad guys figured out their enemy.

So many thoughts. Come on, Willow, sleep! Willow flipped over from her left, then to her right and stared at the clock on the nightstand. It read 9:28. If felt more like one in the morning. She reached for the TV remote and resigned herself to fall asleep the way she used to so long ago—watching old reruns. In reality, this may be the last time she could just relax and enjoy the time. She pushed up against the headboard and hit the remote on button.

Yes. She luckily found an old *I Love Lucy* episode. Lucy had a job packaging candy. As the candy came out of conveyer belt with great speed, Lucy started eating it. Willow giggled. This just may be the perfect distraction.

Helena sat up.

"Oh, no. I'm so sorry. I didn't mean to wake you," Willow said. "I was just trying to get to sleep. I can turn it off."

"Nah, I wasn't really sleeping. Who could? It is way too early, and there is so much happening." She pushed her pillow behind her back. "Besides, it's Lucille Ball. Who doesn't like her?"

"Agreed."

"It feels good to laugh." Helena winked.

"I was just thinking that, too."

And the reality was, they needed it. No one doubted the wild adventure they were on, just like Laura's note had implied, was just beginning.

Chapter Ten

Laura's mind whirled with possibilities and haunts. Who was this enemy? Could it be S.I.U. again? Part of her doubted it. It felt different. But if not, then who? She laid a towel on the shag carpet and began to knock out one hundred push-ups. She had just turned over to do sit-ups when her husband peeked over the side of the bed.

"What are you doing, hon? It's three in the morning."

She dropped onto her left elbow to face him. "I think better when I work out."

"What does it take for you to sleep better?"

Good question. Laura smiled, leaning up so he could kiss her. "Peace and tranquility where all the world is right and full of rainbows and unicorns and lots of dark chocolate candy."

He laughed. "Good luck with that."

"Yeah." Her heart ached from all that had transpired the last twenty-four hours. Why did all this keep happening to them? Leaving S.I.U., bringing down Greenstone and then Harding, all of it was supposed to give them a normal existence. Instead, once again, they were lost, broken, unsure of the future, and this time, even unsure of their enemy. "Maybe I'll go for a run."

Bryce sat up shaking his head. "Um, no, you aren't. It's the middle of the night."

"Are you afraid someone will jump me?"

"Yes."

Laura raised an eyebrow.

"Hey, look at our track record. It is possible the great Laura Black-Chappelle could be taken, or worse, taken out."

As if. Putting her hands on the floor, she flipped up onto her feet and crossed to grab a baseball hat from the dresser. "I think I can take them."

"I'm sure." He slid out from the sheets to join her and wrapped his arms around her waist. His strong muscular body made her reconsider going anywhere.

She kissed him slowly and then met his gaze with a fake pout. "You don't seem to have faith in me."

"If you haven't noticed, my dear, our new enemy is good at kidnapping without any warning. None of us should be alone. Not even the great Laura Black-Chappelle."

"I'll take my ankle gun and a knife." She winked, pushing away to grab both.

"You know it isn't a good idea." Reaching for a white T-shirt on the back of a chair, he added, "Which is why I'm going with you."

"Really?"

He laughed. "Really."

****

The air outside was hot and muggy. The rain had finally stopped falling, but the summer heat held the moisture in place. The Arizona landscape was barren, and twinkling lights from the city ended, leaving pitch dark splotches on the horizon. The two of them jogged in silence for a while, with only the air leaving their lungs sounding in the hushed dark. The cement sidewalk eventually turned to dirt as they ran into the empty desert.

"Where do you suppose we are headed?" Bryce respired.

"I figured we'd just run for about a half hour and turn back." Laura picked up the pace a bit. "Come on, let's burn off those burger and fry calories."

"No, I meant the team," Bryce labored to say. "I meant, where are we going? We just drove all day from San Francisco, and now, here we are in Podunk, Arizona. How far is far enough?"

That was the reason she couldn't sleep—no answer to that question. It made her sick. Suddenly, a cramp clamped onto Laura's side, and she stopped short.

Bryce ran past her and then stopped. "You okay?"

"Yeah, just a cramp. Let's walk back." Clutching her side, she took a deep breath and turned toward the lights ahead. "The truth is I don't know how far we should go. We have an invisible enemy. I have no idea how to fight them. What's even worse is not knowing who we are fighting. I cannot keep us safe if I'm this confused…"

Tears choked her throat. She reached for her husband and stopped to cry on his shoulder. Honestly, she was beaten. Long ago, she felt enough was enough. This was beyond enough. "I can't do this anymore, Bryce."

His hand sifted through her hair. He kissed her forehead and then looked her in the eyes. "If anyone can do this, it *is* you. I know it's a lot. When this is over, I am going to take you to some island somewhere to disappear. Just you and me, forever."

"I love you, you know."

His teeth glowed in the night as he flashed his sexy smile. "Good thing I feel the same, huh?"

"Yeah." Their lips met, soft and inviting. They kissed for a few moments before they started back, shuffling forward on the dirt path. A rustling sounded to their left as something dove into the bushes. Both turned. A hawk screeched somewhere above. Both laughed, and for a moment, the pain was gone. But that was a fleeting second before all the sorrow returned.

When they hit cement, Bryce stopped and turned to her. "When I was overseas, there were many times I didn't know who my enemy was. The terrorists would hide behind the innocent. Women and children were sent forward with bombs. We learned to trust no one. It was a disheartening feeling." He tucked a strand of her hair behind her ear. "But we learned from the mystery. There are always tells. Something that always helps you figure it out. Call it a sixth sense or observation. We will get to understand this and then know how to fight it. We always do. But running will never help us. We can't learn from an enemy in our rearview mirror. We learn from them when we stop to observe."

No doubt, he was right. Laura nodded, grabbed his hand, and led him back to the hotel room. "Where should we hole up?"

"Like always, somewhere desolate."

****

The alarm on her phone buzzed some ridiculous song Charlie had picked to wake her up. Funny, Laura didn't even remember setting her alarm. Maybe Bryce did when they got back. She yawned as she turned it off. Sunlight streamed through a crack in the curtain. Life buzzed around the hotel with sounds of kids at the pool as a maid cart rolled by, followed by several suitcase wheels moving down the sidewalk outside. Laura patted the pillow next to her. *Empty.* She sat up, rubbing her eyes. "Bryce?"

The bathroom door was open. She walked to it—also empty. On the end of the bed was a pair of jeans. She pulled them on, ran a hand through her disheveled hair, grabbed a hat, and walked to the door. Peeking outside, she saw the SUV still parked in front. Maybe they were holed up in another room. She walked back in and grabbed her phone, texting the team in a group chat.

"Room 105," Bryce texted back.

Laura shoved the phone in her back pocket and headed to Charlie and Eri's room. Everyone was there. "Planning time?"

"Eating time," Teddy said.

Willow laughed. "It's always eating time with you."

"We're going to walk to the café for breakfast," Charlie said to Laura. "We didn't want to wake you. Bryce said you had a hard time sleeping last night."

"Did he?" Laura glanced at her husband with mock disdain. Not that it mattered. Her team was an open book. No secrets.

Despite the rain the day before, the short walk to the café was warm and dry. The desert had soaked up the moisture like a parched sponge. A warm breeze swirled to their left, causing a mini dust devil.

Charlie held open the café door, clanking its bell against the glass. The group filed in to a curved booth in the far back corner. The room was filled with a lot of truckers and a few families. A loud hum of voices and the clinking of dishware set the milieu for the room.

After ordering an insane amount of coffee, eggs, breakfast meats, and pancakes, Laura called the meeting to order. "Okay, we need to agree on what is next. I know it's been a while since we had to make this decision, but we're here again, and it needs to be made."

Everyone shifted one way or another in the booth, no one speaking at first. It was not lost that this one hurt. They had all liked their time in Northern California. Many of them got real jobs. Two of the three couples were now married. Laura hadn't told anyone, but she was also pregnant. That hurt the worst. How did she raise a child in this life? That was the real reason she couldn't sleep. If Bryce knew, it would change things. He would look at her differently. Coddling, hiding, no longer taking charge—Laura needed to be in control. She wasn't ready to be the *pregnant female* who had to be protected. Was that selfish? Maybe. She would deal with those feelings later. Right now, she just needed to get this done. Get her family to safety. Fight this enemy. Start over.

"Maybe we should leave the U.S.," Helena said.

They all knew she was ready to go back to Puerto Rico, to find her sister, and return to some semblance of her life before, but that would never be an option. The last time they chose to return down there, it about killed them all.

"We can't go back, Helena."

"I didn't mean to Puerto Rico. We could go anywhere...Canada...Mexico. Somewhere, not here."

That had merit, but to what end. "I think we need to stop and figure out who we are running from," Laura said.

Bryce nodded. "Just hiding will not help us. We know from experience we cannot outrun our enemy. We don't know their resources. They may know we're here now. Are we even safe? We have no idea at this point."

Of course, he was right. But that didn't help them figure anything out.

Teddy pushed his empty plate away and burped.

"Gross," Helena said.

Everyone laughed.

"Hey, burping releases those endogenous toxins, that seep into your bloodstream, from your body. If you hold them in it can be dangerous to your cells and digestive track."

"I agree," Myers said, before letting out an even louder burp.

Helena gave him a dirty look.

"What? Just protecting my digestive track and those erroneous toxins, per Dr. Teddy's advice."

"Endogenous," Teddy said.

"Po-tay-toe, Po-tah-toe."

Smiling, Laura looked over the rim of her coffee cup and stopped. A young Latino kid in a gray hoodie stood at the cash register with a pistol aimed at the waitress. He spoke in hushed tones. Laura placed her cup on the table and nodded to Myers, who had the best site advantage. "You distract, I'll unarm."

Myers nodded as he eased out of the seat.

"Everyone focus on Myers, not me," Laura said. Why didn't they bring their guns with them? Maybe it was for the best. No need to start a shooting match with this many civilians in the place.

The rest of the group followed Myers with their eyes. He walked to the edge of the booth as Laura leapt behind the counter. A napkin holder sailed through the air, landing just feet beside the assailant. The guy turned his gun toward where Myers had been and yelled, "Stop or I'll shoot."

People screamed and began scrambling under tables.

Myers must have popped back up, because what sounded like silverware hit the counter.

The kid fired a shot in his direction and glass shattered. "Nobody move, or I'll shoot everyone in here!"

Laura peeked back out. Myers was under the table, safe, offering her a thumbs-up sign. She edged back around behind the counter low to the floor.

More screaming, some crying.

"Just give him the money," someone yelled.

Looking at the reflection in a napkin holder, Laura could see the kid had his back toward her. Placing her hands on the counter, Laura flipped over and kicked him in the head. The gun slid across the floor. The kid fell to the tile, dazed. Myers retrieved the gun. There was a moment of silence, and then, everyone began to clap. Laura spun the kid over so he was facing the floor and pulled his wrists together behind his back. "Do you have any duct tape or string?" she asked the waitress.

The cook came around, mouth open, eyes wide, and handed her an apron and a knife.

"Thanks." She cut off the straps and glanced back at the cook. "Call 9-1-1."

"Already did."

The realization of that made Laura act fast. They couldn't be here when the police arrived. In some ways, they were still wanted, and any inquiry could put them all in jail. Fingerprints and fibers put them in the proximity of at least half a dozen murders, maybe more, not to mention all of them were supposed to be dead. No way did she want to explain this. How did one explain they weren't bad guys? That everything was either self-defense or ridding the world of filth? The law would not understand. Robin Hood was still an outlaw, even if his intentions were good.

She knotted off the string and pushed him up against the side of a booth. Blood ran from his nose, and a dark circle appeared just under his left eye. He couldn't be more than fifteen. Not long ago, this was Myers. She glanced at her friend holding the gun. "Sorry, kid, but this wasn't cool."

The kid began cursing at her in Spanish. She didn't know all the dirty words, but she recognized a few. She put a finger to her lips and leaned forward. "Sshhh," then whispered in his ear, "I could snap your neck without breaking a sweat, so I suggest you settle down, my friend."

"Lo dudo," he spat at her.

With a sneer, she moved within an inch of his face, "You doubt it? Darle una oportunidad."

His eyes widened when she called his bluff. She pulled back and peered at her team, all hovering nearby. "We need to go."

Myers wiped the gun surreptitiously and handed it to the cook. "Keep it on him until they arrive."

"Don't you need to be here when the cops come?"

the waitress asked. "You're witnesses."

Laura shook her head. "Unfortunately, we can't. It would ruin our cover."

The waitress smiled, chomping on her gum. "Are you some kind of undercover cops or something?"

"Yeah, something like that." Laura patted her arm. "I'm glad you're okay, but we've got to go."

Within seconds, the sirens blared a block away. The team hurried toward the exit. The roomful of people clapped and cheered, but they didn't stop to gloat. Once outside, each of them set out in a run. The red and blue lights were now visible on the horizon. Not much time. Each person entered his or her room. Laura and Bryce began grabbing everything and tossing it into their two duffel bags. Two minutes tops, they were at the SUV, ready to go. This was not a new exercise. They had lived it, as well as practiced it. Always running, they got pretty good at it.

"Go to the left," Laura yelled to Myers. "The police are pulling in on the right."

With a hard swerve, Myers sent the vehicle around the building and down the dirt road Laura and Bryce had jogged just the night before. No telling where they would end up, but there was no time to figure that out. They just needed to get free of another good deed gone wrong.

Chapter Eleven

Teddy waited until the dust settled, and they were back on a main highway to pull out his phone. He inserted his earplugs and began to scroll through some of his favorite social media sites. *Oh no!* His face went white. "Pull over!"

Laura glanced back from the passenger seat. "What's wrong?"

He turned the phone around so she could see the screen.

Her eyes went wide. She snatched the phone from him and unplugged the earplugs. "Myers, pull over!"

"What is it?" Deshawn asked.

Laura passed the phone around as Myers exited the freeway. He drove into a gas station lot, shut off the engine, and faced her. "So?"

Holding the screen so everyone could lean in and view it, she pushed play on a video. The scene from the café played out as it had occurred. Already, the moment of Laura slamming the kid to the ground had over 12,000 viewers. Teddy couldn't believe it. Anonymity had been their one friend. The idea of people recognizing them would not bode well. It would draw out their enemies and put a target on their backs—especially with the law. Laura had said as much many times. Never be seen. Never get caught. Leave no identifying traces.

"What do we do now?" Teddy asked. "I mean, the chances of this thing going viral around the world with over millions of viewers will make it impossible to go anywhere. Of course, these things usually die out, and the team wasn't seen right? That's something."

"Yes, luckily, the video didn't show the rest of the team. Just Myers and me. It is quite the set back, but not impossible to maneuver. The two of us will have to lay low. The rest of you will have to do all the shopping and negotiating." Laura handed Teddy his phone back.

"It's not a big deal. I can hack the account," Charlie said. "But I agree we need to lay low, since some people have seen it, especially in this area."

"We need to stop just driving and have a plan. Where are we going, Black?" Myers said with more bite than probably needed.

"Helena said it earlier. It's time to leave the country." Laura bit her lip and then said, "Head for the border."

****

It was dark when they approached two signs that read: "Bienvenidos a Mexico" and "Nogales Centro." This wasn't the border Teddy remembered in Tijuana. It seemed more desolate and not as heavily guarded. Maybe that was a good thing.

"Passports out," Laura said.

Everyone started to pull them out, just as they reached the booth. A security agent motioned for them to roll down the window. Charlie, now driving, complied.

"Where are you going?" the guard asked.

"To a wedding in Oaxaca, Mexico."

"Do you have any firearms, food, or drugs within your possession?"

"No, sir," Charlie said.

"Passports, please."

Teddy's hand sweated as he dug his out of his boot and handed it to Charlie. Everyone also passed them forward. The man leaned in and checked each of their faces against the faces on the IDs. "You will also need to obtain a permit for your vehicle. Cost is $27. You can pull through over there." The man passed the passports back to Charlie and pointed with his other hand to a white building.

"Thank you," Charlie said and then maneuvered over to park. "Please tell me this car is registered to one of us."

Laura reached into the glove compartment and handed out a white slip of paper. "Yes, it's actually under Myers' name." She passed it back. "Go on. We'll wait."

Helena jumped out and joined Myers on the other side. Holding hands, they crossed to the side window. Laura had taught all of them that whenever in these circumstances, it was always better to go as a couple. It seemed less suspicious and more normal.

Charlie stepped out to of the vehicle and took the seat where Myers had sat before. "Just in case, he should drive."

"I had you in the driver's seat, because Myers may be a wanted man. I just hope there are no issues inside." Laura glanced to where he had disappeared behind a brick wall. "His face was on that video."

It seemed to take forever for them to return. With each second, Teddy felt more paranoid. Though it was a bad habit, he began biting his nails. So many ideas swirled through his imagination. What if they figured out who Myers was and had arrested him on the spot? What if any moment a S.W.A.T. team would surround them? He imagined helicopters and rifles pointed at their car, police dogs, riot gear, CS Gas, and bullets.

In an instant, they would take him away and lock him up forever. Or worse, shoot him for no reason. They were at the border. What if there was no due process? What if they lied and said they were armed? Well, actually, they all were—guns lined the roof of the car. Most people looked under the car or the floorboards, few people thought to look at the roof. At least, that is what Laura had said. So, they specially lined the top with an entire arsenal. Charlie was a great actor. *Did they have firearms?* Teddy tried not to laugh. *They have no idea.*

Teddy glanced at the ceiling, wondering if he could get to them fast enough in the event the guards surrounded them. He played the scenario out in his mind a dozen times. Hit the hidden button. The case drops down. He grabs. He shoots. Could he do it fast enough? His mind replayed the mental practice over and over. Movement to his right made him jump and, instinctively, reach for the hidden button. But luckily, he didn't press it.

Myers and Helena rounded the corner.

Teddy visibly exhaled.

"You okay?" Willow asked, touching his elbow.

He nodded. "Overactive imagination."

She smiled. "Yeah, me too. Just knew the guards would surround us at any moment."

"I went as far as S.W.A.T."

She giggled. "Of course."

Myers settled in and started the car. Within a few minutes, they were back in the line of traffic, moving toward the last rim of American soil.

Once across, Teddy yelled, "Viva la México."

Everyone laughed.

"Indeed," Deshawn said.

The traffic was thick and moved slowly. Little children ran to the car dressed in rags and no shoes. Withered, sundried, elderly men approached the car with towels and squirt bottles. Women balanced hats and scarves on their bodies and on sticks. Myers kept inching the vehicle forward. It broke Teddy's heart; how he wished he had the money to help all of them.

"Drive about an hour, then find a hotel," Laura said.

"Sounds good." Myers finally broke free of the crowd, and the pace improved. Windows rolled down, and the warm air blasted them, lulling Teddy to sleep. When he opened his eyes, they had stopped outside a bright orange and forest green building with a hand-painted sign that read, "El Pequeño Motel—Vacante." Dust swirled around their car as everyone opened their doors in unison. A chicken cackled at Teddy's side and ran behind a shed. A thin dog chased after it, being stopped by an elderly woman with a broom. "Pero, no!"

"Hola." Laura put on her best smile. She always became sickly sweet in these situations. It made Teddy wonder if they all really knew her at all. One might call her a chameleon; she had a face for all circumstances.

"¿Hola?" the woman countered, looking at them suspiciously.

"Nos gustaría estar aquí esta noche," Laura said.

"What did she say?" Teddy whispered to Helena.

"She is trying to get us a room."

"Gotcha."

The lady wiped her hand on her apron and then put her thumb and index together and rubbed the universal sign for money. "452 pesos."

Laura turned back and looked at Charlie. "How much is that?"

"About $25."

"American dollars?"

"Sí."

Laura handed out the money. "Sí, nos gustaría."

The woman took the money and then motioned for them to follow her. She lifted her red poplin skirt as she stepped up the two steps into the building. Inside, it opened into a brick-colored tile courtyard filled with potted plants and ceramic jugs. She led them to the other side and stopped at an orange door. Opening it, she waved a hand out for them to enter.

"Isn't big enough for all of us," Myers said.

Laura glanced back to the woman and waved at the room, then held up two fingers. "Dos?"

The woman shook her head, then one finger. "Uno."

"It will have to be," Laura said, moving toward the opening. "Gracias."

"Denada."

The seven of them stepped in the room with just one queen bed and a fold out cot. "This will be a tight squeeze," Willow said.

"Yeah." Teddy grinned and pushed into Willow, pretending he had to step closer to her.

"Bien?" the woman asked.

Laura nodded. "Baño?"

The woman indicated the restroom was around the corner, then shuffled back down the way they had come.

"It's just for the night, or until we figure out where to go," Laura assured. "Charlie, fire up the computer. We need to plot a path."

Chapter Twelve

Laura tried to flip over softly to avoid waking the other two women who shared the bed with her. The men all slept on the floor, with the exception of Myers on a cot by the door. Not sure how he scored it— probably rock-paper-scissors or a flip of a coin. Or even more likely, to keep his snoring to a minimum. She smiled and then exhaled slowly.

Need to quiet my mind. Please fall asleep, brain. Often tightening each muscle, then relaxing it, she could begin to doze, but not tonight. *No such luck.* The uncomfortable arrangements, Myer's buzzing breath, the other sleep noises, the humidity, and the lack of planning were all recipes for insomnia, which seemed to be occurring more and more. When was the last time she actually just fell asleep? Like always, maybe it was time for a run. She tossed her feet over the side of the bed and patted the ground for her tennis shoes.

"What are you doing?" Bryce whispered from the floor, a hint of amusement in his voice.

"What do you think?" She pushed her foot into one shoe, then the other. "I'm going running." She reached for the thin hoodie she had used as a pillow.

"I thought we agreed running alone is stupid."

"You're welcome to come again, though I also keep reminding you I can take care of myself."

"Maybe, but it still isn't safe." The sound of him shuffling around told her he was getting ready, too. In a way, it would be nice to spend time alone with her husband. It hadn't been easy. They needed this.

The air outside was oppressive. The buzz of mosquitoes and tree frogs set the music for the run. The moon hid to a small sliver, not offering them much guidance. She adorned her head with a flashlight and handed one to Bryce. He flipped it on and placed it on his head.

For a while, the only other sound in the night was the patter of their feet on the dirt road. The wildlife seemed still. Every once in a while, a soft breeze would blow, giving them a hint of relief. But for the most part, it was thick air—like sludge to their lungs. About a mile out, something rustled to her left. She turned her lighted head to the sound but could not make anything out.

"Do you see anything?" Laura asked, turning back to Bryce.

A red dot marked his chest.

"No," she screamed.

A loud bang shattered the still air, echoing off the mountains. Laura tackled him to the ground. Warm, sticky blood covered her chest.

"Bryce," she cried. "Stay with me, sweetheart." She flicked the light off and scanned the dark horizon. Tears blurred her vision, making it hard to see. Silvery figures moved to her left. She grabbed a pistol from her back, aimed it, and then fired. Fired again. Both shots hit something metal. Lights turned on from what looked like a truck. It peeled out; its tires spinning in the dirt. In seconds, only dust was left in its place.

Laura turned back to her husband. "Bryce, speak to me."

"I lub you," he gurgled.

Sobs ravaged her body. She tried to clear them, to think. Pulling her phone from her back pocket, she dialed Charlie. "Come on, come on."

"Hello?" Charlie mumbled.

"Bryce has been shot! It's too dark to do triage. We're behind the motel about one and half klicks away. I need you to bring the SUV now."

"You got it." Charlie hung up. She called him, because out of their entire team, he would respond the quickest through the emotion. He could still function when he felt things. Well, at least, unless it was Eri.

"Stay with me, Bryce. Please. I need you." She pulled off her T-shirt, leaving her in only a sports bra. Rolling it up, she thrust it against his chest.

The sun had just begun to wink at the horizon when Deshawn, Charlie, and Myers drove to her location. They quickly picked Bryce up and placed him the back. Laura climbed in the opposite door and placed his head in her lap. It looked like the bullet was just right of his heart. Fear gripped her own. This could not be happening. Why him? Silently, she prayed for a miracle. How she needed one now.

They pulled up to the motel, and the entire group was ready to receive him. They had plastic trash bags on the bed, ripped rags, hot water in pots, bottles of alcohol, a burned needle, a knife, and thread all ready to go.

When they placed him on the bed, Laura was sure it was too late. Bryce's face was ashen, his lips blue. No breath filled his lungs. Helena went to work on him.

During their downtime, she had been training as an EMT just for this reason. Each of them had tried to learn a new skill. This one seemed the most apropos.

Helena started with CPR. It seemed to bring him back, even if for a moment. Then she went to cleaning the blood. There was so much of it. "It was a through and through. That's good, because then I won't to have to dig out a bullet." She cleaned him up and poured alcohol on a warm towel and tried to treat the wound. "Myers can you flip him, so I can get the other side?"

Myers and Deshawn helped.

Helena then worked to sew him up, her hands visibly shaking.

Bryce winced. That was good. He was alive and felt pain. Laura would take it.

After Helena was done, she stood staring at her bloody hands. Myers escorted her out of the room, probably to clean up in the shared bathroom outside.

Eri and Willow removed the bloodied bags and rags from the bed, pulled a chair from the patio, and placed it by Bruce.

"Sit," Eri said to Laura.

She nodded but barely felt herself slide into it. Every extremity felt numb. How did this happen? Was it their enemy, or was it the Cartel, or was it someone else? The moment of the bullet hitting replayed over and over in her mind, like a sick animated GIF to her psyche.

This was once again her fault. Why did she have to go running? He knew there would be danger. Always did. Guilt encompassed her, followed by a chaser of grief. She reached to hold his hand. It was cold, lifeless. "Please, honey, you have to live. You're all I have."

Outside, a scream pierced the night.

Willow and Helena ran to the door, just as Myers ran in.

"They have Deshawn."

Laura jumped up. "Who, who has him? What happened?"

Tears pooled in Helena's eyes, as she tried speak. She croaked, getting nothing out.

"We went in the bathroom hut to clean up. I heard a car drive up outside. I didn't think too much of it, until I heard her scream," Myers said.

"Myers?" Laura looked at him.

"We entered the bathroom. Something slammed against my head." He took a deep breath and continued, "I fell backward against the sink. I heard Helena scream. The room was spinning. Everything was a blur. I was trying too hard to clear my head...to stand...to see what was happening. When I finally got my bearings, she was gone. For a moment, I thought they took her."

Helena shook her head. "These two masked men came out of nowhere and grabbed Deshawn from the porch. It happened so fast."

First Bryce, now Deshawn. Wait, no first Willow, then Eri, then the men. Who were these people? Why are they just targeting one of them, and not killing all of them? "They are trying to break us."

"What?" Myers asked.

She paced, shaking her head, and then stopped in front of her tall friend. "Whoever is doing this...it isn't just about killing us. It is about tormenting us. That is why they took Willow, then Eri, then shot Bryce, now Deshawn."

"They aim to hurt us emotionally." Helena touched Myers' arm. "We're next."

He visibly swallowed and pulled her into him. "You are not leaving my sight."

"But why Deshawn? He doesn't have a girlfriend here."

"He's muscle. First, they take out Bryce, then him. I would say Myers is next."

Myers stepped forward with a scowl on his face. "Laura, I think this is about who you care about. They haven't gone after you. Just everyone around you."

The thought had occurred to her. "I'm sorry everyone."

He wrapped an arm around her. "I didn't say that to hurt your feelings, I just think we need to acknowledge it."

She nodded, fresh tears pooling in her eyes.

"What do we do about Deshawn?" Eri wiped a hand over both her tear-stained cheeks.

Laura was torn. She wanted to go get him, get their friend, but didn't want to leave Bryce. "We have to go get him, but I need to be with my husband."

"No, go," Bryce whispered.

Laura fell to her knees by his side. "You're awake?" New tears trickled down her face, falling to the mattress. "I thought I lost you."

"Not yet. Too tough for that." Lightly, he touched her hand.

She laced her fingers with his and leaned to kiss his cheek. "I'm not leaving you, okay?"

"They need you. You know they need you. No one ever fights or thinks like you."

Helena came to her side. "I can stay. You know

Myers and I will be the next target. It isn't safe for us to be together anyway. I can stay here, dress the wounds, and make sure he has food and water."

"Are you sure?"

"Absolutely. I can speak the language, so it should be no problem at all."

Laura leaned over her husband and whispered in his ear, "What do you think?"

"I think you should go," he whispered back.

"You know I love you and that dying while I am gone is not an option. If you truly love me, you'll still be here when I get back." She kissed his cheek. "I have something I need to share with you when I return, and you need to be lucid to hear it."

"Understood," he said with a genuine smile.

She kissed his lips this time and then stood to face the room. "Then let's go get Deshawn and kill anyone with him."

Chapter Thirteen

Helena paced in the room, waiting for the call. Claustrophobic from the metallic smell of blood in the hot room, she opened the door and stood on the small veranda breathing the outside air deep into her lungs, though the humidity outside did little to help. She glanced around. With the exception of a Yucatan bird nipping at cracks in the ground, the courtyard was empty. Finally, her cell rang, and the light gray and yellow bird took flight.

She answered and had her orders. "Understood."

This would be the hardest day of her life. She loved Myers. At some point, she began to need him. And she cared for most of these people on some level. But all of this was bigger than Myers. This was bigger than her feelings. This was about true family. Her heart might hurt for a while, but as Alicia always said, men were like buses—another would come along eventually. Helena walked to Bryce's side and stared down at him. His breathing indicated he was still asleep. In a moment, that would certainly change. It would be good to make sure he couldn't fight back.

She withdrew a syringe from her bag and walked back to his side. She stuck the needle deep into his neck. His hand started to rise. Eyes opened. Then both relaxed. Her heart thundered in her chest. No going back now. Grabbing a pillow, she straddled him and placed it over his face. Instantly, even despite the drugs, he started to thrash violently. Using every muscle she had, she fought his body's need to survive. Just when her muscles began to fail, his body went limp. She pulled the pillow off and touched his neck. No pulse. She put a hand on his chest. His breath ceased to move. The deed was done.

A huge part of her soul seemed to seep out onto the bed. This was harder than she ever thought possible. But it was necessary. Breaking Laura had always been part of the overall plan. It became apparent, almost immediately, that as long as Bryce was in her life, Laura could endure anything. That needed to change. It began here. Now. Today. At the loss of her lover, Laura would finally die inside, and then, they would crush her.

Staring at his lifeless body brought a range of emotions. Sadness was one of them. Though the team would now disagree, she wasn't a monster. Internally, she began to rationalize all she had done. After all, there were sound reasons—ones that only some would understand.

When her boss decided to leave Helena with this group, he warned her she might fall for Laura's "family"—love them even. He said loyalty was a tricky thing but keeping it in check was another. She assured him. There was no doubt; she knew where her loyalties lay. It was not with this makeshift family that was always running from ghosts. Her loyalty would forever be locked to those administering payback for her dead father.

Helena turned from the body and dialed Alicia.

"Yeah?"

"It's done." Helena's voice shook. She cleared her throat. "Now what? Do you want me to join you? Get rid of the body? Leave it? What?"

"One sec." Alicia's voice became muffled, as she was likely talking to their fearless leader. After a moment, she came back on. "We don't think you should be pulled out just yet. It may be better to be the mourning friend for a while. We might be able to get her sooner that way."

Disappointed, Helena glanced back to Bryce's body. "Fine, but this corpse is going to smell nasty in this heat. I think if I bury him, it would be better. Then it will also cover any trace of foul play."

"Agreed."

"And Deshawn?"

"He's tucked away nicely."

"Okay. Be safe. These people are no joke."

Alicia laughed. "Neither are we."

The phone went dead, and Helena went to work. Moving the body ended up being quite the chore. Bryce had to weigh twice as much as she did. Using the bottom sheet as a catalyst, she dropped him from the bed, then dragged him outside, through the courtyard, and around the back of the building. The sun was high, and the temperature was scorching hot. Perspiration saturated her back and face as she tugged him to a remote space in the vast desert. Every once in a while, his head would bounce on a rock, and she cringed. A few buzzards called and circled close to her position. Her muscles squealed for her to quit. This had to be far enough.

She laid him straight and then began collecting

rocks to cover his frame. Though her body felt weak and tired, she didn't stop. Each rock became heavier and heavier, but this had to be done before they returned. The entire task must have taken two hours. Desperately, she needed water and rest. *Just one more thing to do.* She fashioned a cross out of two sticks, weaved it together with the stem of another plant, and then pushed it at the top of the rocks.

"I really am sorry, Bryce. You were a super nice guy. You just picked the wrong woman to love." She took a step back, kissed four fingers, and touched it to the rock. "Vaya con Dios."

In the distance, a vehicle bounded toward the motel. *Oh no, they're back.* She sprinted for the room. Inside, a bloody stain ran the length of the bed. That would be their problem to clean up. She grabbed a water bottle from the small fridge, drank until it was empty, and then relaxed in the chair, trying to still her rapid pulse. The moment in front of her would need to be the best acting job of her life. If any one of them suspected foul play, there was no doubt she would join Bryce in the desert.

The SUV stopped outside, and Helena mustered some tears. Within seconds, Laura traipsed in. Instantly, her smile fell, and her eyes went wide. She stared at Helena for an explanation.

Helena bowed her head, pretending to cry. "I am so sorry, Laura, I really am."

"Why? Why are you sorry."

Helena met her worried eyes. "He didn't make it."

"What? No," Laura screamed and buckled to the floor, her body wracked with sobs.

The group, minus Deshawn, ran in one behind the

other. All looked to the bed and then to Laura. The reality of the situation came to them quickly. Myers began to cuss and then hit the wall creating a two-inch hole. Helena had the ability to calm him, but she couldn't. Not this time. This was on her. The villain. The hypocrite. The monster. How could she console anyone when she felt so retched?

Charlie left the room with hands cupped behind his head.

Willow and Teddy knelt to Laura's side, trying to console her.

"What happened?" Myers asked.

Helena mustered some tears—some actually real. This was not easy. Call it fear or conscience, her eyes watered. "All of a sudden, he just stopped breathing." Not a lie. She could sell that. "I buried him in back. I knew in this heat... he would... it would make him start to—" She stopped. That wasn't a statement that could be finished. "I can take you to him, Laura."

Laura nodded and tried to stand on what appeared to be wobbly legs.

Willow and Teddy came on each side of her and helped her walk. Together, the team staggered to the makeshift grave. For a moment, no one talked.

Finally, Myers spoke. "This isn't right." His voice choked, "I'll miss you, man. You were like a brother."

Laura opened her mouth, but no words escaped.

The other few said their thoughts, memories, and goodbyes; Helena heard none of them. Her mind was too far from what was happening. This moment filled her with a weird sense of evil, making her seem inhuman. Out of body, she felt numb—maybe it was her way of disbanding any conscience.

"What do we do now?" Myers croaked through tears.

Laura used his shoulder to stand and wiped her face on her sleeve. "We find whomever is responsible and return the favor."

Helena stared at the floor, afraid to move, scared to look up, knowing that right now, her expression would not save her from this wrath.

Chapter Fourteen

Laura stared at the rock grave, saddened to her core. One side of her could melt into this desert and lay her life next to her husband's. The other desired revenge, and if they were trying to break her completely, they failed. Half of her still lived, and it was fueled, ready to kill. That would be the feeling she would give in to. It would propel her forward, like it did Myers when he lost Denise. She glanced behind her, and their eyes met. He understood. His loss was fresh in his mind, too. Together, they would see an end to this hidden enemy. No more being their mouse. It was time to bring their own claws out and hunt them down.

"Myers, can I see you a moment…alone?"

He nodded and followed her farther out into the desert. The rest of the team seemed to watch, but slowly returned to the building. Helena was the last to go, maybe waiting for Myers, but eventually, she left too.

Once they were gone, Laura fell into his arms and sobbed. Hard. Wrenching. Her body trembled, as she gasped for breath. He held her tight, stroking her hair, and she could tell he cried with her. Finally, when she could cry no more, she pulled back. "Sorry, I just needed a friend."

His own eyes moist, he nodded. "Always. Never apologize."

"I need to tell you something, but you have to promise not to judge me or stop me no matter what happens."

He touched her shoulder, concern in his eyes. "You know I've got you no matter what. Bryce was my boy, and I will look out for his wife."

Yes, and that very reason was why they needed to have this conversation. Once the group knew the truth, he would definitely be the one to try and stop her. "Myers, listen. I need you to promise me that you will not try to stop me from going after these people, no matter what I'm about to tell you."

"No matter what." He held up three fingers. "I want this just as bad as you. I've got you. Scouts' honor."

"Were you even a scout?"

He shrugged. "For a millisecond, yeah, sure."

She stared at him a moment, her heart racing. It was hard to push the news past her lips. "I'm pregnant."

His eyes remained on her, vacant without response, as if they didn't seem to compute her words.

"Did you hear me?"

He nodded, mouth open, obviously dumbfounded.

"Say something."

"For real?"

"Yeah, for real."

A huge smile spread across his face. He grabbed her and pulled her into a hug. "Congrats, Mama. Did Bryce know?"

She shook her head and stepped back. Fresh tears slid down her cheeks. "No, I had planned to tell him tonight."

"You waited so he wouldn't stop you."

This man knew her well. "Yes."

"And that is why you made me promise not to stop you."

She paced around him, kicking at a rock. "I need this fight, Myers. You know that more than anyone. These people just killed the father of my baby and the man I loved. They will pay."

"Okay."

"Okay?" She looked to him, surprised.

"Yeah, you know I love you guys. That baby deserved a father. This is personal for me, too." He cleared his throat from emotion. "You do what you've got to do. I'll be with you every step of the way."

"There is one more thing."

Myers folded his arms in from of him and nodded for her to continue. "Don't tell me twins."

"Hardly." She wrinkled her brow. "No, something is wrong here. Tell me you sense it, too."

He tilted his head sideways, obviously trying to understand what she meant. "How so?"

"Don't you find it a bit strange that this enemy is somehow finding us? That they know where we are at all times?" She paced a few feet, hands on hips, allowing her mind to fill with possibilities. "We are continually careful. Always have been, and yet, they know us—where we will be, even when we are all alone in the middle of nowhere." Spinning on her heel, she spanned her arms out to encompass the vast empty backdrop. "Look around, Myers. Why would they come here? To Mexico? Somehow, they are always waiting. Watching. Ready."

He studied her before speaking. "Are you sure that last night was the same people from before and not cartel?"

She stepped closer and looked him in the eye. "I would not be alive. They would have checked. This felt personal."

His head dropped, sending his focus to an open hole at his feet. He kicked the dirt, not speaking, but apparently thinking. She waited. Maybe she was crazy and needed his voice of reason, not that Myers was that voice to her. But with the exception of Bryce, she had always trusted Myers more than anyone else on her team. He had always been loyal. No way would he lie to her or give her smoke. Whatever he said, whatever he thought, he would share with her honestly.

"I agree. Something isn't right." He glanced over his shoulder, back to where the group had disappeared behind the building. "Is it one of us? I have a hard time believing that, but could it be?"

"Hopefully not." They were close—family—but then, her training and experience always gave her pause. Often the enemy was closer than most thought. Harding had proven that. "But if so, I don't know which one. Willow was kidnapped, and you saw Teddy's response. I don't think that boy could do it even if he wanted to, and why would Willow do that to herself?"

"Right." He nodded and strode a few steps away, then faced her. "And everyone else has been with us since the beginning."

"Not everyone." Laura gingerly met his gaze, knowing the implication would not set well.

"I trust her with my life, Laura." With chest out, he took a step toward her. "No way Helena is involved. Move on."

"Okay, maybe not. I hope you're right. But, this

enemy knows us…personally. We have got to stop running and figure this out." A beetle ran onto her boot. She pushed it aside and reached out to touch Myers' arm. "I need you thinking with all cylinders. Paying attention to everything they do. All are open to scrutiny. Do some of your computer stuff. The sooner we know our enemy, the sooner we can begin to fight them."

"Okay, I will. But I don't like spying on our friends." He put a hand on hers and squeezed.

"I know." She hugged him again and sighed. "But something isn't right. Let's get back."

They walked the rest of the way in silence. She knew Myers would not like her accusing Helena. But she needed him considering it as a possibility. Though she doubted Willow and Teddy had anything to do with this, there was always the possibility they could have been turned.

Willow was with the enemy for more than twenty-four hours. Maybe she wasn't really in danger. They never checked to see if the claymore mines were functional. And Teddy, maybe his joyfulness was a ruse. Maybe he wasn't working at the movie theatre all those months, but rather, he was meeting his handler. And then, there was Helena. She was alone with Bryce when he died. Not to mention, she had been with her pseudo family a shorter period of time.

Memories of the first time they met came to her memory. She had fired a gun at Laura's head and then she turned them into the enemy. So, who knows? Not the best history. And where is Alicia? The girl just disappeared. Should they consider she could have been following them? All of them were suspects until she could determine otherwise.

Kimberlee R. Mendoza

90

When Laura entered the hotel room, it had been cleared and cleaned. The group sat around, quiet, reflecting, obviously lost in their thoughts. She sat on the floor next to Eri and laid her head on her friend's shoulder. Eri responded by wrapping an arm around her. Charlie joined on the other side. Together, they wept. That day was the longest day, but it was also the last time Laura wanted to give into this feeling.

"We need to know our enemy. It is time to stop running and start fighting," Laura said, wiping her tears with the back of her sleeve.

Myers squatted in front of her. "You know I'm all in."

"But what about Deshawn?" Helena asked. "Did you guys get any idea what happened to him?"

Laura sighed. All of this had completely made her forget their friend was missing. "My hope is that when we find them, we'll find him, too."

Eri squeezed her shoulder tight. "We all are in. So, what do you want us to do?"

Chapter Fifteen

Helena heard something through a fog.

"What?" Helena blinked against the hot sun.

"Are you okay? I've been yelling your name?" Myers stood over her, hands on his hips. "I was trying to see if you could stay back while we go scout."

She nodded.

"Great, see you later tonight." Myers kissed her and then joined the rest of the crew in the SUV.

Sure, why not? I am always good for staying back, fetching supplies, whatever is the least threatening adventure. If this were a real relationship, where she didn't have to play nice, things would be way different. Often, she was overlooked. Her thin frame and diminutive statue made her appear weak and innocent. Both were hardly true.

She had scored extremely high on her IQ test, was the equivalent of a black belt in martial arts, and could toss a knife at any target with exact precision—not that she would ever let this group know that. It wasn't the plan. She had almost given herself away back at the cabin last year when she fought Laura. Harding would not have been happy. But all of this made her ill.

Always endeavoring to establish she was better than everyone else was a constant battle and put her on Harding's radar in the first place. After a bar fight went wrong, she ended up in a Mexican prison. There she met Alicia—a younger girl with a big attitude. Like her, she looked about five years younger than she was. Most thought she was maybe fifteen, but in reality, she was twenty-one. She never told anyone the truth. Her mind flooded with memories of the last year and all that had happened.

Alicia and she were recruited by S.I.U. for one purpose—to destroy Laura Black. At first, it seemed simple enough. Helena was sent to shoot Julio and hang out there until Laura appeared. Harding assured her Laura would come. To this day, she still wasn't sure why that worked. He said it had something to do with a "dog always returning to its vomit." *Gross.*

But it was prophetic. Unsure why, but she did come. Pretending to fire on Laura and Bryce and miss was hilarious. In seconds, both of them could have been dropped by her hand. However, Harding commanded they were to be taken alive. The plan was for Laura to kill Greenstone and then join them. Amazing how most of it fell into place. The crew's suspicion was short lived, and Helena and Alicia were officially on the team.

Helena shifted on the ground and drank from the water bottle in her hand. Nothing was perfect. In some ways, it backfired. Unable to get word to Harding about the final raid, S.I.U. fell, and he was captured. Thankfully, she suggested the mental institution, as it was likely easier to break out of than jail.

After the smoke cleared, Alicia went back to free him. It took much longer than they thought to get him out, but once they did, everything was back on. Together, the three of them began to torture the *Black*

Squad, as they had begun to call them. The idea was to kill off their team one by one until the only one left was Black. Still harboring a grudge for locking him up, Harding wasn't sure if he would kill her yet, thinking it would be better to let her live with the pain.

But killing everyone on the team had been harder than they thought. Twice, they had failed. It wasn't looking good—until today. Helena sighed. Bryce was dead—the one who would hurt Laura the most. If his passing was all that happened, it may be enough.

Helena turned on her phone and dialed Alicia.

"Yeah?" Alicia said.

"They're gone. Are you extracting me?"

The sound muffled, and Alicia spoke away from the earpiece. "Are we getting her?"

Harding came on the line. "I'm not sure that is the right play. It helps having you there."

"If you take me, they will think you kidnapped me and come looking for you. It's the perfect scenario." She took a deep breath and let it out slowly. "Plus, it's been almost a year. I can't do it anymore."

The line was silent for a moment. "Fine. Meet us latitude 24.02775 and longitude 104.65319 in two hours."

"Okay. Thanks." Helena rumpled through her stuff, seeing if there was anything she couldn't live without. Then grabbed her passport and a GPS, tugged on her boots, pulled her hair in a ponytail, and donned an olive-green cadet hat. A knife sat on a small table by the door. Helena cupped it in her hand and willed herself for the next part. Big breath in. She lifted her pant leg and cut an inch slice. Blood ran down her calf. Scooping it up, she smeared a handful on the counter, down the wall, across the bed and pillow, and ended with a few drops by the door. She kicked a lamp, shattering it across the room, and then pulled the blankets from bed. That should do it.

She glanced around one more time and headed out the door. In the distance, she could see a billow of dust. *That could be them.* No time to waste. Helena took off across the desert, GPS in hand. A part of her felt sad. This had not been the best day. Though she signed up for this long-term assignment, knowing she would betray them, it still stung a little.

There were some real feelings for Myers and even for Bryce. That probably hurt the worst; it pained her to kill him. But it was the job. The hate for Laura was real. All of them had been indoctrinated to despise her—some through hypnosis, some through suggestion. For Helena, her hatred came from one very important reason. Her real father, Ignacio Perez, had been murdered by Laura's hand five years ago.

Tears pooled in her eyes, blurring her vision. Helena blinked to clear them. The memory of that night was still fresh in her mind. She had just received news she had been accepted into an American university. Excited to share the news, she ran up the stairs to her house, whistling. But then stopped. Something was not right. The lights were all off, and the front door was slightly open. A stream of blood smeared through the entryway and down the hall. At the end of the trail was her father. She deduced shot in the back as he tried to escape with a final kill shot to the head.

For three years, she tried to find the killer. No one knew who until that night when she was arrested. Harding knew. He showed her the case file, where

Greenstone had ordered the hit, and Black had carried it out.

Helena sniffed and wiped her face with the back of her hand. From then on, whatever he had in mind, she was his girl. No matter what, this would happen. Often, it was hard. At times, she actually started to like Laura. But one flash of memory from that night, and all the feelings returned. It took everything in Helena to stick to the plan. Several times, she had had to restrain herself. One night, she had actually stood over Laura's sleeping body with a knife in hand. If Bryce hadn't rolled over, she would have stabbed their leader in the heart.

A pebble rolled under foot, causing her trip. She grimaced as the dried blood on her leg separated from her jeans. *How much farther?* She glanced down at the GPS. *Almost there.* The sun beat down hot burning her nose and exposed arms.

Almost there. Something shiny shimmered in the distance. *A vehicle, maybe.* She squinted to see it in the bright landscape. *Yes. A truck.* She smiled through parched lips. With arm extended high, she began to wave. "Hey!"

The truck circled around and gunned its engine, before driving to her spot.

Alicia leaned out the side window and waved back. "Hello, my sister. Ready to do some real damage."

"I'm just glad to be free." Helena smiled. "Could use some water though."

"Get in." Alicia opened the door and shifted over the seat, sitting in the back. A Hispanic guy Helena had never seen sat at the driver's wheel.

"Hola," Helena said, climbing in.

He nodded and revved the engine.

"This is Gael." Alicia handed her a canteen. "He doesn't talk much, but he's got mad fighting skills. He's the one who nailed Bryce with that bullet." Alicia patted his arm, then turned to Helena and pointed at her leg. "You're bleeding. What happened?"

"I left them a gift." She winked and took a long drink. When she pulled back, she said, "Better they think I was hurt."

"Smart." Alicia leaned forward and folded her arms around Helena's neck. "This is going to be so fun."

"How's Harding?"

Alicia sat back, licking her lips.

"Alicia?"

"He's good. There might have been a slight development."

Helena tried to turn around in her seat, but the belt kept her from going far. "What?"

Alicia stared out the window, a slight smirk on her face. That infuriated Helena. Even though they didn't really share DNA, they had been partners for three years. Often, they fought like sisters. And right now, Helena was in no mood for the girl's game. "What happened?"

Her head slowly turned to face Helena, the joy of what she was about to say plastered on her expression. "We hooked up."

Helena's eyes went wide, and then she grimaced. "Gross. He's like, how old?"

Alicia crossed her arms, obviously determined to fight that resistance. "Um, only twenty-five. Remember, I'm twenty-one, not fourteen like the crew thought."

"Fifteen."

"Whatever."

"You hooked up with the boss? I thought romance was forbidden in S.I.U.?"

She shrugged. "It is. But he's in charge and makes his own rules. Besides, this whole thing is rogue anyways."

Helena glanced out the windows and watched as cracked earth scattered with yellow bushes rolled by. Inside, she knew this was not sanctioned, but pretending it was made it easier to complete.

"It's about revenge, Helena. About all of us getting our due." Alicia slid the window behind her open and stuck her hand through the opening.

That Helena could understand. That she could appreciate. Laura killed her dad. Until she had suffered enough, Helena would be Harding's puppet. That was one thing she would endure. When it was over, maybe she would kill him, too. How else would she find true freedom? It was about using people to get what she wanted, right?

Chapter Sixteen

Teddy turned down another empty road. It had been hours, no sign of anything useful. "How much longer do you want to do this?"

Laura leaned forward in the middle. "I don't know. I hate that we not only lost another one of our men, but also any sign of the enemy."

"I'm starving," Eri said from the back. "I say we call it a night. I think we'll be better tracking them in the morning. The sun is already starting to set."

"I'm with her," Charlie said.

"You're always with her." Laura laughed. "Fine, you're probably right. Go ahead, Teddy, turn it around."

He didn't have to be told twice. As soon as he could do a U-turn, he did. The trip back took another half hour, and his stomach complained for food. "I hope that tamale truck is still open."

"Ooh, that sounds awesome," Charlie said.

Teddy pulled in the lot and cut the engine. He stepped from the vehicle, drained. His usual busy mind felt subdued through a fog of sleep, such an emotional day. He didn't know which he wanted to do more—eat or sleep. He trudged through the courtyard toward their digs, nudged open the door, and gasped in disbelief. Any fog swished away. The room was in disarray.

Blood covered the walls, the bed, and the floor. He opened his mouth to scream, but no noise escaped.

The crew entered laughing and stopped in unison, all halting at the door, shock present on their faces.

"Where's Helena?" Myers pushed past Teddy, frantically glancing around the room. "Whose blood is this?" He lifted a pillow traced with blood. "No! No, this is not happening. Where is she?"

"We need to follow the blood trail." Laura snapped a flashlight onto the floor, then walked out toward the back of the building. "The sun is beginning to set. We have to hurry," Laura yelled over her shoulder, breaking into a run.

The group quickened their pace. Everyone followed, heads down, except Myers and Teddy. Myers' fixed stare was on the horizon; Teddy's was on Myers. He had experienced Myers' rage before. It was how his friend dealt with grief. No lie, it could be frightening when he got super mad. Something like this could send Myers over the psychological edge. After all, he lost his first girlfriend to a bullet. Could he have lost another the same way? Teddy's heart ached for this man and Helena. He silently prayed it was not how it looked.

No one spoke. Teddy wanted to say something. Nerves usually made him prattle, but something told him to keep quiet. The eeriness of the forlorn desert made the condition of this so much worse. Myers charged out in front. Anger and pain evident with occasional grunts. After a few miles of tracking blood and footsteps, they spotted tire treads and Helena's trail went cold.

"The trail...it ends here. Whoever took her,

stopped here to grab her," Myers said, pacing with hands cupped around the back of his head. "This can't be happening. Who would take her?"

"Well," Laura sucked in her bottom lip. "Don't get mad, but I'm not convinced she was taken."

"What?!?" Myers head snapped up as he glared at her. "Of course, she was. Don't be absurd."

Laura pinched her lips together, studying him for a moment. Teddy understood her hesitation to speak her mind. Nothing she said would change the outburst that was sure to come. "Myers, as you know, I've been doing this a very long time. You have always trusted me, right? I have never led you astray. Not once. I have nothing to gain by doing so." Her tone was patronizing, but she was obviously worried about what she had to say next. "To be honest, I don't know why it didn't click before, but this just confirms it. Helena was the spy."

Myers walked toward her with a puffed-out chest and fire in his eyes. If he swung, Laura would take him, but it would not be pretty to watch. "Stop lying, Black. You know that isn't true."

"Listen to reason, Myers. There is just one set of footprints until this point. There was no fight or struggle here. We know that, if she were taken, she would have not gone easily. Whether or not we like it, she walked out here on her own and got in this vehicle willingly. If someone was chasing her, we'd see a second set. If someone abducted her, there would be signs of a fight, a skirmish, a second set of prints." Laura lifted her hands to her face and rubbed. "Even back at the hotel, there was no sign anyone was there but her. No sign of other footprints but hers. And…"

Tears were evident on her cheeks, and her voice cracked as she said, "I think she killed Bryce."

The group visibly gasped together.

Myers stepped away, shaking his head, clearly angry. Tears began to crescent his eyes. He flipped around, violently wiping at them.

"Why would you say that?" Eri asked.

"Bryce was fine, and then he wasn't. And then, she buried him without letting me see him one last time. I think she covered up the evidence." Laura lifted her head, blinking. "She's been playing us since Puerto Rico."

"No!" Myers spun around with more hurt than rage in his voice. "No, I refuse to believe that. She loves me and wouldn't do that."

Laura closed her eyes. It obviously upset her heart to speak about this. "I know that's what you need to think, but I've done the same con several times, Myers. It isn't hard to gain one's trust—to pretend to love someone. If you don't know to look for it, a good agent can be very convincing." She joined Myers' stare. "Look, she even had me fooled, and that is hard to do. I was trained to pick those kinds of people out. So, once I know what to look for, it is like a string being unraveled. It comes apart quickly, and the individual pieces are revealed. It doesn't matter if we want to believe it or not, she was a spy."

Myers stormed off, but slowly paced back.

Eri squatted to the ground.

Charlie hovered over her with a hand on her back.

Teddy didn't know what to do. Helena was family. She had been a friend. Never once had he suspected anything but loyalty to their cause. Now, Alicia was a different story. Often her behavior had been unpredictable, bizarre even. When she left, it hurt him. Maybe Laura was right; she was teamed up with Helena this whole time. "Do you think Alicia was in on it?"

Laura glanced at Teddy.

Eri stood with Charlie by her side.

"Yes, I do." Laura nodded. "That's why Alicia left. Everything started happening shortly after her departure."

Teddy raised his hand, as if he was in school. "Um, guys, I have something to tell you."

They all huddled around him, their eyes curious.

"The night before she left, I found her in the basement doing something odd. I am not sure what, but when I started to confront her..." He swallowed, trying to get this out. "She kissed me."

Willow's eyes went wide. "Oh my gosh."

"What?" Laura faced her.

"Is it that strange she would kiss me? I mean, I know I'm weird, but seriously it's not that—"

"Teddy, I meant Willow."

"The voice of my abductor." She stepped forward. "At the time, I was trying to pick out the strange accent. I felt like I knew the voice somehow. It was Alicia. She's the one who held me."

Laura sighed. "I was afraid that might be the case. Look, we all need to rethink things. Every moment you were with them, analyze them. You will see them differently now."

"This is ridiculous," Myers mumbled, his gaze steadied on the dirt floor. He obviously was not taking this well.

Laura came alongside him and whispered

something in his ear. He seemed to soften some, but not much. Without Helena, could Laura control this wild beast? It didn't seem likely. Teddy made a mental note to avoid the man.

"What do we do now?" Eri asked.

Laura met each of their gazes one by one. "We find them, and we end this."

Chapter Seventeen

Laura lay on the dark cot. Her face warm and wet from tears that would not stop falling. Her mind wandered from memories of Bryce to Helena the day they met.

Laura and Bryce made their way up to Julio's bamboo home. Instantly, Laura knew something was definitely wrong. The door was slightly ajar, and a dining room chair lay upside down on the porch. The two of them glanced at each other. Just coming from the airport, neither had a weapon. Guarded, Laura slid the door open with the toe of her boot. On the floor, between the living room and kitchen, Juan's corpulent frame lay in a pool of tacky blood. Laura ran to his side and checked his neck. It was cold and hard. He had been there for a while. A maggot ran across her finger. She shook it off and wiped her hand on a nearby kitchen towel.

A gunshot rang from the adjoining room.

Bryce fell back.

Laura screamed, "Bryce."

"I'm okay." He touched his left shoulder and looked at his hand. A dot of blood appeared. "It just nicked me."

Both scanned the room. They needed weapons—now.

Laura low crawled to a drawer, slid a paring knife to Bryce's side, and then reached for a utility knife. Not elegant, but it would have to do. She indicated with a nod of her head that he'd take left and she would take right. Another bullet pelted the wall behind them. They ducked but kept inching forward. Laura mouthed with fingers held high, "Three, two, one."

Both jumped through the door and tackled an olive-skinned woman to the ground. The gun rattled to the floor next to Bryce. The woman fought, but they managed to wrangle her onto her stomach, pushing her head into the dingy beige carpet.

"Alto!" She screamed.

"She wants us to stop," Bryce said.

Laura rolled her eyes. "Yeah, I'm sure she does."

"You're American?" The woman's voice was muffled by the dirty shag carpet.

"Yes."

"I'm sorry I shot at you then."

Laura rolled her over, but straddled her, keeping both arms above the girl's head. "What do you mean?"

"I am Julio's daughter, Helena. The men from the village, they came and killed my father. He did nothing wrong. My father said to wait for an American woman."

Laura locked on Bryce's gaze. She had no idea what that meant. He shrugged. She looked back to Helena. "You're assuming he meant me? Why?"

"He said Laura Black would save me."

Laura cringed at hearing her name. "How do you know I am Laura Black?"

"I've seen a picture." The woman rolled her eyes up, indicating something over her head.

A photo sat on a small dresser behind her. In it, Laura smiled with Julio. She didn't remember that picture being taken. Nor did she understand what was happening. It had taken a lifetime to build a "trap meter," but Laura had one. "How could your father assume I was coming? I didn't know he was in trouble." Laura glanced at Bryce, making sure he caught her meaning.

"Suspicious," Bryce mouthed.

Why hadn't they stayed with that premise? She also gassed them, stating it was to save her sister. Also, as Bryce said, *suspicious*. They brought her into their group. Protected her. Trusted her. And she killed the man Laura loved. Everything in Laura's body wanted to find her, place a gun to her head, and fire. So much rage and agony radiated throughout Laura's body. She didn't know what to do with these feelings.

A hand touched her shoulder. For a brief moment, Laura thought maybe it had all been a bad dream. Bryce was there, holding her.

"Can we talk?" came Myers' voice.

Laura opened her eyes and sat up. "Okay, but not here."

They stepped over bodies and exited the room. The air was still humid. The only light came from the moon overhead. Myers lit a small candle and placed it on the veranda. Both sat on ground, with their backs against the wall of the building.

Myers pulled her into him and together, they cried. Bodies shaking, distraught, so much pain washing through tears attached to fallen lovers. "It is hard for me to accept this. I waited so long to allow Helena in. My heart still belonged to Denise. But I cannot deny what you are saying. I was closest to her, and I saw the signs. I just refused to admit them. That would, in some way, tarnish Denise's memory...to move onto someone else like that. I just couldn't concede—"

Laura touched his face. "It's okay. We'll be okay." They were nice sentiments, but in this moment, they landed like lies. How could they be okay? Either of them?

She pulled back and noticed his freshly-shaven head. "What happened to your dreads?"

He half-smiled. "I left them on the bathroom floor."

"You know Charlie is going to tease you mercilessly."

"I would expect nothing less."

Laura leaned her head on his shoulder. For a moment, neither talked. A slight breeze blew, sending a sweet aroma of what smelled like lavender their way. She closed her eyes, trying to find peace, but doing so only made her wish Bryce was there.

"Who do you think they work for?" Myers asked.

"I think I have an answer," Charlie said from the open doorway. "Sorry if it seemed like I was eavesdropping, but I worry about you both."

"It's okay. What do you have?" Laura said, sitting up.

Charlie folded to the ground with laptop in hand. "Harding was released from the mental institution the same week Alicia disappeared."

"What?" Myers grunted. "Then it is true? Alicia was part of this? And Harding is pulling the strings."

The news was a gut punch. Laura knew what Harding was capable of. "Now that we have all the pieces, all of this is making sense. Go with me." Laura faced them, just as Eri joined the group. "Harding wants Greenstone killed. So, they set us up in Puerto Rico, knowing I would kill him the first chance I got. Then Alicia leads me back to Julio's place. Helena does the same. They convince us to take them with us, and they are in."

"But we took Harding down and killed their dad," Eri said.

"Not their dad." Charlie shook his head and spun his laptop around so they all could see the screen. A news clipping with two younger girls were displayed under the heading, "Niñas Que Falta." *Missing girls.* "I did a little digging now that we know what to look for. Helena and Alicia weren't related to Julio. These were his daughters, fourteen and sixteen. They disappeared a week before he died."

That confirmed it. It just made the angst worst. Laura glanced at Myers. His lips where puckered, his eyes down. Slowly, he lifted his gaze to meet hers and nodded. He was in. They would fight this war together for Denise and Bryce.

"So, what now?" Eri asked.

"Let's try to get a few more hours sleep, then we stop being the prey and begin to be the hunters." Laura used Myers' shoulder to stand. "Night."

Each returned to the room. There was no guarantee that any of them would sleep. Teddy and Willow were out, but maybe this didn't go as deep for them. They never knew Denise and had only known Bryce for a little over eight months. Or maybe it was because Teddy could always find a silver lining. He was their own personal Pollyanna. Hopefully, this would not tarnish him. Death had a way of hardening the heart. It did hers so many years ago. Only Bryce had softened it enough to create this family.

Focusing on the memory of his face, she closed her eyes. It didn't happen right away, but eventually, her mind relaxed, and she fell asleep.

****

"Let's get moving." Laura tied off her boot and stood.

As the team packed up, Teddy prattled on. "I was able to talk to Miguel, the owner's son last night, and he told me all sorts of cool trivial. Like, did you know that Mexico... It's actually called Estados Unidos Mexicanos, which means United Mexican States, which is interesting, because we are the United States of America. So, we are both United States. I never really thought about that, have you? Anyway, he also told me the first printing press was actually used in Mexico City in the 1500s, and they have a tamale called a zachuil that weighs one hundred and fifty pounds."

Laura usually loved the enduring quality of their youngest family member, Teddy, but today, it was boarding on obnoxious. It was not lost on Laura that he chattered more when he was nervous or anxious. This likely qualified, so she tried to endure it. No reason to hurt his feelings because she was in a bad mood.

"I think I've heard that," Laura said dryly.

"And did you know that millions of monarch butterflies migrate to Mexico from the U.S. and Canada every year? I guess they are like birds, flying south for the winter, though there isn't much winter in the south, so I wonder. But it is interesting. I have always liked them, especially the color. I'm fond of that color orange." He peered slightly at Willow, who blushed when she apparently realized he was talking about her red hair.

Despite herself, Laura smiled. Maybe his talking was distracting them. That could be a good thing. "What other Mexican trivia did you learn talking to the owner's son?"

"I'm glad you asked." A big grin spread across the blond boy's face. "Did you know that Mexico City is actually built over the ruins of an ancient Aztec city and a lake? And because of that, it is sinking like six inches a year?"

Within ten minutes, the SUV was packed. Eri and Charlie used bleach and rags to remove any blood and fingerprints, and Willow collected any apparent DNA. Better it appeared they were never here. When the room was spotless, the crew boarded with Myers at the wheel. Charlie sat next to him with laptop in hand. Helena had made one mistake. She still had her cell phone, which meant she could still be tracked.

"So, where is she?" Myers said.

Chapter Eighteen

Myers rubbed a hand over his now bald head. Though everyone chided him last night for shaving off his dreads, it was time and almost therapeutic. The immediate future would not be easy. He pulled out of the lot, ready to do whatever it took to avenge their family members. Harding was ultimately responsible, but the girls were not innocent. They would pay. After a long drive, Charlie pointed to a skinny dirt road that led to what looked like a border crossing.

"Are we going back to the States?" Laura asked, leaning over the seat.

"It's where the tracker is taking us," Charlie said.

"I don't like it."

Myers glanced over his shoulder, then back and forth from the road to Charlie. "Do you think it is a trap?"

"That is always the first thought." Laura glanced at Charlie's screen. "Where does it stop?"

"El Paso."

"They're in Texas?" Myers asked.

The road dropped down a hill, and then, the U.S. border came into view. The contrast from the close-boxed homes of Mexico to the spacious houses and buildings across the border were clear. They would soon be back in the U.S.A.

"Passports out," Laura commanded.

Everyone readied himself or herself. Anytime they had to go over the border was scary. Technically, they were all fugitives, but the good news was no one knew who they were. Someday, that could change. It would only take one smart cop and a bit of modern technology to find them. Anyone with skills like Charlie or Myers could crack the code on this family. It all depended on how important they were to the FBI. After all, Charlie did hack the FBI last year; not to mention, Black's family had killed hundreds of bad guys. Even though they paid for all the damages and stolen goods, they still committed many robberies and crimes.

"Keep it slow," Laura said, as they approached the line to cross.

A Border Patrol Agent stood just outside a hut speaking into car windows and then either waving them through or to the side. It took a good thirty minutes, but eventually, it was their turn. Myers accelerated forward and rolled down his window. "Good afternoon, sir."

The agent peeked in the car and met every eye. "Where are you coming from?"

"We attended a funeral just outside Mexico City," Myers said. It wasn't a lie. Laura always said it was better to tell as much truth as possible. It prevents eye dilation and other physical tells.

"Where do you live?"

"San Francisco."

It was almost a truth. It is where they lived before.

"Passports."

Everyone passed them to Myers who handed them to the agent. He looked at each photo and then returned it and asked, "Are you bringing anything into the

U.S.?"

Each said no. Finally, he handed the last one back and waved them through. A verbal sigh could be heard throughout the car. They were back in the U.S. and not in prison.

"Did you know the Mayans used to throw what is called a hornet bomb at their enemies?" Teddy said, breaking the tension. "Seriously, they would take a hornets' nest and chuck it at them. I hate anything that flies and buzzes, even more if there is a stinger at the other end."

The space was silent for a moment, until everyone began to chuckle, then laugh, and then roar. It was a much-needed release. Whether tired, broken, or just relieved, they laughed for a good ten minutes. Tears rolled down Myers' cheeks, only these were laughter induced. He could barely see the road.

"We're close. Turn at the next light," Charlie said, bringing the mood back down. "The signal is about a block away."

All laughing stopped, and the tension resumed.

"It's a trap, right?" Eri said from the back seat.

Laura glanced at Myers' stare in the rearview mirror. "Likely."

"So, what do we do?"

Myers slowed the car by a curb and put it in park. He turned to face the group, and Charlie did the same.

"We need to do recon and not be half-baked this time. Let's watch the house. Get some surveillance in there." Laura glanced at Charlie. "Do you have any of those tiny drones still?"

A big smile lit up his face. "Yeah, two."

She shifted around to look at Eri. "You ready to go

114

ninja with me?"

Eri nodded. "Sounds like fun."

"We'll wait for it to get dark. Myers, go *shop* for a less conspicuous vehicle. We'll stick out like agents if we drive up the street in this thing." Laura glanced at Charlie. "You do what you do." Then she twisted in her seat to see Willow and Teddy. "You're backup. If anything happens to Eri or me, you take them down."

Now with marching orders, Myers stepped from the vehicle. The summer weather was balmy—a little cooler than Mexico, but not by much. He grabbed a baseball cap from the floorboard and slammed the driver's side door closed, probably harder than he should.

In the past, Helena was the one person who could calm his anger. Now, she was the cause of his fury. There was nothing holding him back. That scared him. How did he refrain from the fire inside? Not wanting to disappoint Laura or the team was all that held him from walking down the street and raining bullets on Harding and his girls.

Once again, loss lay heavy on his heart. Losing Denise was not like this betrayal. Only a few months ago, he'd given himself completely to Helena. The idea of marrying her someday began to enter his mind. The only thing that stopped him from marrying her was the memory of Denise wanting the same. *Praise God for that.*

An old, green '80s sedan was parked in an alleyway. In the window was a for sale sign. He pulled his phone from his pocket and dialed the number. It had taken six months to pay everyone back from the last time they traveled across America. This time, they were trying to stay legit. S.I.U.'s payout kept them well off enough; they didn't have to steal much anymore.

"Hi, I was inquiring about your Granada. How much?"

"Ya'll want that thing?" the man on the line said with a thick southern drawl. "My old lady was gonna sell it for $500. It just ain't got no tags since it took so long, and we couldn't sell it." He yelled to someone else. "Mildred, someone is asking about Buck." Myers could hear a muffled voice, and then the man came back on. "I'll take $100 to get it out of our alley."

"I'm at the car. Can you meet me?"

"Sure thing. One moment. I need to put on some pants."

Myers laughed and discontinued the call. It took the man about twenty minutes to appear. The few strands of gray hair he had stood up on end. He wore overalls and no shirt. Behind him was an oversized lady dressed in flowered housecoat.

"Howdy." The man stuck out his hand. "I'm Ray. This here is Ola. So, you want to buy Buck?"

"Is Buck the car?"

"Yes, sir. She runs fine, just can't pay to get her tags done. We don't go far nowadays. No need for a car. They wanna tow her, and I'm about ta let 'em."

Myers reached in his back pocket and pulled two hundred dollar bills out. Somehow, he felt the need to overpay. "Here."

"This here is $200."

Myers nodded. "Yeah, I feel I should make an honest deal."

"Well, I'll be. You got yourself a car, young fella." Ray stuck out one hand for a shake and held keys in the other.

Myers shook his hand and took the keys. "Thank you again."

"No, thank you. Y'all ever need somethin' you just let me and Ola know."

"Appreciate it. Night." Myers unlocked the door. The hinges squeaked as he climbed inside. The seats were a little worn, but overall, it didn't look too bad inside. However, it had a slight mildew and oil smell. Myers placed the key in the ignition and turned it. It backfired, but then purred. He pulled the door closed, waved, and started back to his friends. Ray and Ola waved behind him, grinning ear to ear. So much darkness surrounded them; it was nice to bless someone for once.

Chapter Nineteen

Laura low crawled to the back porch. No longer could she view Eri. It didn't matter. Right now, all focus needed to be on not dying. Harding would anticipate her coming. Traps would be set. Even if he thought they were well hidden, he would still plan for this. A camera, snipers, and some sort of reconnaissance was likely in motion. They would be fools to think this was all a surprise. With that in motion, she would try to be aware.

Like a cat, she slunk up to a window and rolled over to look through a crack. Empty. She waited, listening. Nothing.

Eri buzzed in her ear. "No sign of anyone. Are you sure this is it?"

"It's where Helena's phone led us. We need to get inside. Charlie, anything?"

"Yeah, go ahead and release the drones," Charlie said. "Any opening...a doggie door, cracked window, whatever you can find. You are clear to have them enter."

From what she could tell, there weren't any holes or openings. Laura glanced up to Eri, who stood above her on the roof.

"Fireplace." Eri nodded higher.

Laura tossed the mini drone. Eri caught it, back

flipped to the top of the brick stack, and dropped it in. "Now, Charlie."

"Check your phone."

Eri bounded back to her side and peered at Laura's screen. The drone flew around the house. Each room was vacant. On the kitchen counter was a cell phone. "I think we found it."

"Are we clear to go inside?" Eri asked.

"Let me check the rest real quick." The drone passed into a back bedroom, a few bathrooms, down a hall, up some steps, and into a few more rooms. Finally, it was deemed empty, and hopefully, free of any booby traps. "Okay, but please be safe."

"Thanks, Charlie." Eri laughed. "Because we were going to be anything but."

"Man, my wife is sassy."

Eri chuckled. "Quiet, so I can be safe."

Laura fiddled with lock until it clicked. She turned around, walked to the yard, squatted to the ground, picked up a handful of dirt, and then returned to the back door. "Walk softly, be very aware."

Eri nodded.

Laura tossed some dirt in the air. No laser. She walked forward, her eyes darting from corner to corner. Every step creaked in resistance, making her heart beat faster. She reached the phone, grabbed it, and motioned for Eri to back out. They were almost back to the door when the phone rang. Both women visibly jumped.

"Are you going to answer it?" Eri asked.

Should she? It was no mystery who was on the other end. Laura slid the bar, pushed the green button, and placed it on speaker. "Yes?"

"Good to see you found the phone, Agent Black."

It sounded like Alicia. "I guess the jig is finally up. You now know with whom you are fighting."

"Alicia? Why? I thought we were family."

She snickered. "Have you ever considered what all those orders over the years did to people, Black? Did it ever occur to you that you were killing innocent people? People who had families, loved ones? That somehow you were making enemies and not even realizing it?"

"You know I never killed anyone because I wanted to. I was only following S.I.U. orders just to stay alive. Same as you."

"Ha!" The phone was silent for a moment, and then she said, "Have Eri leave, or we'll shoot her in the head right below the brim of her black hat."

Laura glanced at Eri. She was indeed wearing a black hat which wasn't super unusual, but it did give Laura pause. It was highly probable they could see her.

"You're probably wondering if we can see you. Face any way in the house, and I'll tell you what you are looking at."

Adrenaline began to fill Laura's body. She turned to her left, now facing a cat picture on the wall.

"Good. You're looking at an orange tabby cat. Ugliest picture I've ever seen, but we didn't decorate the place. Shall we try again?"

This time, Laura faced the sink, looking out the window.

"Tricky. You turned to the sink, but your eyes are focused on the window."

Laura motioned for Eri to return to the car.

Eri mouthed, "What about you?"

Holding up one finger. "I need to finish this call—

alone."

Though not quick to obey, Eri finally exited.

"What do you want from me?" Laura asked.

Alicia laughed again. There was something evil in her tone, menacing. It sickened Laura. How could this be the same girl who had lived with them for over six months? But then, Laura knew. She had played a long con before. It took a lot of acting skills, but it was not impossible to fool someone. Harding handpicked Alicia for a reason.

"You want to know what I want from you?" Alicia laughed. "I want you to die, Agent Black. Not today, of course. That would be way too easy." The screen door behind Laura flipped open, and Alicia stepped out with a gun. "No, you need to suffer for your crimes. Down on your knees, Black."

"You are not going to get out of here with me alive. You know I'm not alone."

Alicia looked at her sideways and sneered. "Please. And what? You think I'm here alone? This entire house is surrounded by the best S.I.U. has to offer. We were never in this house. We took residence in the houses around this one. Waiting. Hoping. Praying, even, that you would fall for our precious trap. Of course, you did. You are so predictable."

Myers appeared behind Alicia. Laura tried to pretend she didn't see him, but some micro expression must have given it away.

Alicia elbowed behind her. Myers swung and hit her in the jaw. Laura went for the gun as it slid across the room. Alicia leapt, too, but Myers yanked her back by her hair. Laura grabbed the gun. Alicia kicked her hand, causing Laura to drop it again. She was just about to rush for it when the door opened revealing Harding with a gun to Eri's head. Helena held a gun to Charlie's head.

"Now here we all are…one big happy family." Harding smiled. "This is quite the reunion. But wait, we're missing a few from the original group, aren't we?"

Red faced with clenched fists, Myers ran toward Harding.

Just inches away, Harding cocked the gun at Eri's temple. "Ah ah ah. You wouldn't want to put a bullet in another friend, would you?"

Myers backed off, but not without spitting at Harding's feet. He began pacing like a cornered animal; his eyes filled with disgust. If Myers saw a crack, Laura knew he would take it. This could end in a blood bath.

"What do you want, Harding?" Laura said, trying to calm the situation.

He tilted his head sideways and gestured the gun around the room. "It's what we all want, my good friend. Justice. Closure."

"What does that mean?" Eri asked.

"It means, my waif enemy, that everyone in here is tired of playing these games with your crew. It is time to end this once and for all. Helena?"

Helena stepped the rest of the way into the room, a sardonic grin plastered on her face contrasted with what appeared to be tears. Her gaze locked with Myers'.

Hatred seethed through his expression.

Harding laughed. "Awe, the happy couple reunited at last."

"Harding, don't," Helena warned. It seemed there was some conflict happening inside her. A fight between good and evil. It was good to know. Laura may be able to use that.

Circling between Helena and Myers, Harding seemed to gloat. "Agent Luther, do you ever wonder who pulled the trigger on your precious Denise?"

Myers' countenance seethed.

"You see, we had to find a way into your band of outlaws, and you were our best bet. Denise was in the way of our plan." Harding wrapped his arm around Helena's shoulders. "So, I had my good agent, Helena here, kill her."

The room went nuts. Myers lashed out at them both. One of Harding's men took him down with a punch to the throat. Everyone began fighting, but within minutes, Black's family were all subdued with syringes in their necks. Laura saw a few drop before her own body went limp.

****

When Laura opened her eyes, it was dark and damp. A soft drip fell to her right. The smell of mold and sulfur burned her nostrils. Her hands and feet were both bound. A chain rattled when she shook her hands. "Hello?"

Silence.

She tried to focus in the darkness. Without any light, she struggled to adjust her vision or make out any shapes. Worry consumed her. Not for herself, but for those she loved. What had happened to the rest of her team? If Harding's main focus was to torture Laura, they would have no use for the group. *Please, God, protect them.*

Someone groaned by her feet.

Her heart flipped. Maybe they were with her. "Is

someone there?"

"It's Myers." His voice sounded weak.

Relieved, Laura leaned to her knees and did her best to shift to his side. "I'm so glad you're okay. I thought for sure they'd killed everyone."

"I'm a big guy. It took a while for the drugs to kick in. I saw them take Charlie and Eri out, but I'm not sure what happened to them."

"Are you okay?"

"Yeah. You?"

"Thirsty, hungry, and a huge headache, but I'll survive."

"Yeah."

Laura leaned against him. "We have to get out of here. Are your hands in front of you or behind you?"

"Behind."

"Okay, turn with your back to me. Let me see if I can untie you."

It took a few times of maneuvering, but eventually, they were back to back. She felt the bindings. No such luck. "Shoot! Leather straps, with a metal lock. Not going to work."

They shifted back around next to each other.

"We'll figure something out."

Laura pulled her legs to her chest and stepped through them, so her bindings were in front of her. None too soon as her shoulder muscles were on fire. "Step through your arms. It will relieve some of the pain."

Myers grunted a few times but must have complied.

They sat in silence for a while. Laura leaned her head on his broad shoulder and sighed. "I'm really sorry about Denise."

Myers sniffed. "Yeah, it seems Helena killed both of them."

"We're going to get out of here. Alicia, Helena, Harding—they are all going to pay."

"You know, putting them in an insane asylum isn't going to work this—"

Laura cut him off. "No, this time will be different." She closed her eyes. Images of Bryce fluttered through her mind. "This time, they all die."

Chapter Twenty

Teddy ducked down low in the car and watched as a couple goons loaded their friends into two different vans.

Alicia walked out, and Teddy's heart rate increased. He leaned over the steering wheel, trying to read her—to somehow understand the why behind all she had done. She was his friend, maybe even something more. How could she betray him like this? All of them? It stung deep into his soul.

Suddenly, someone ran up behind her. Alicia flipped around and kissed him passionately. When she pulled back, the streetlight illuminated his face. *Harding.* Bile filled Teddy's throat. He swallowed, hoping to keep it together.

"Well, I didn't see that coming," Willow said from behind the passenger seat. "Did you?"

Teddy shook his head, too shocked to speak.

Willow slid over the passenger's seat arm and dropped down in front. "What do we do now?"

"We follow." He stuck the key in the ignition but didn't start it yet.

"I don't know, Teddy. That is a lot of manpower. I don't know if we can rescue them."

Teddy glanced at Willow in the moonlit car. The amber light made her green eyes light up, bright and

126

beautiful. He gave her the best reassuring smile he could muster. "Laura trained us well. We have this. We just have to find the right time."

Right now was not that time. Right now, they had to wait. Too soon, and they would give their position away. His head swam, dizzy. Wow, he wasn't breathing. He sucked in some air and tried to relax.

"Are you okay?"

He shrugged. "Yeah, sure, why?"

"You're not your usual chatty, happy self."

"Our friends are in there. There are only two of us. And my ex-whatever is dating Satan. Not a lot to be happy about right this second, you know?"

Willow laughed and then covered her mouth with her hand. "Sorry. I shouldn't laugh. You just surprised me, and I laugh sometimes when I'm uncomfortable."

Though his instincts said it was wrong to laugh, he couldn't help it. His outburst *was* comical.

"I am sorry, though. For real. Not about laughing, but about Alicia." Willow touched his bicep. "It isn't right."

"Yeah." Teddy glanced at her and offered a closed-mouth grin. "At least now I know who she is...what she is. That destroys any residual feelings, and I can move on." Instantly, he wanted to take the words back. Did she know he meant *her*? In the dark, he prayed she couldn't see the heat rising in his cheeks. In the light, he'd be a crimson tomato. "You know what I mean."

She laughed again, then leaned over, and kissed his cheek. "I know exactly what you mean."

Did she mean what he hoped she meant? As he opened his mouth to respond, the vehicles began pulling out. "It's time."

The last of the cars joined the caravan. Teddy turned on the engine and followed slowly, not turning on the headlights. When the caravan came to the end of the road, one van turned right, the other left.

"Which one do we follow?"

"Eeny meeny miny..." Teddy said pointing to each one, picking the left one, he said, "moe." He didn't know which friend or friends he was following. Hopefully, Laura. She would be the best bet for rescuing the rest of them.

Willow clipped in her seatbelt. "In some ways, this is good. We aren't taking on as many people at the same time."

"True that."

The van drove for about an hour before pulling up to a large red wood barn. A man, dressed all in black, got out of the van and opened the barn door. The driver pulled in, and the man closed the door behind the vehicle, then walked around the side to a smaller door, and disappeared from sight.

Teddy rolled the car behind a clump of trees and cut the engine. "I'm glad Myers picked green for the car...more camouflage. See how many guns we have back there."

Willow climbed over the seat and transferred a duffle bag to the front seat. "Five handguns, a rifle, a few knives, and one CS gas grenade." She passed them out equally, ending with the rifle. "Who wants this?"

"You. I'm better at hand-to-hand, so I want my hands free," Teddy said. "You can fire from a distance, right?"

"Yeah, I'm a good shot. Here." She reached again in the bag and then passed him an earpiece. "How do we want to do this?"

"I'll go around back and see if there is any other way in. Once I have eyes on, you can go in the front door."

"Sounds good." She tucked a gun in her boot and another in the back of her pants. Teddy started to open the door, when she caught his sleeve. "This is dangerous. We could die."

Not lost on him. "Yeah, I know."

She rose onto her knees, leaned over the middle console, and touched her lips to his. They were warm, sweet. Tingles shot through his system. She slowly pulled back and smiled. "It's about time, right? I mean if we're going to die, I want to say I did."

Teddy grinned. "Me, too."

"Good," she said with a deep sigh. "Now that we got that said, let's go kick some bad guy butt."

"Agreed."

Both of them exited the car. The night was silent with the exception of cicada buzzing and clicking in the brush behind them. The two of them moved stealth-like to the end of the building and ducked down. Willow went for the door, and Teddy ran around to the back. A small ladder lay on the side of the red building. He climbed it carefully, engaging all his senses. Inside, two people were strapped to chairs. Both wore hoods. From their short height, Teddy guessed Charlie and Eri. Neither Harding nor the girls were present. Just a couple big guys holding AK-47s. One stood in front of them. Another paced behind.

"Can you hear me?" Teddy whispered.

"Yeah."

"I spy with my little eye a couple of unfriendlies,

both armed, on both sides of our target. Thoughts?"

"We need to draw them out. I'll be bait, you rescue."

"No, I'll—" Too late. Willow instantly started banging on the garage door. Both guys walked toward the sound. Teddy wasted no time. He climbed through the loft window and landed softly onto a pile of hay. Without hesitation, he slid around to a ladder and shimmed to the ground below. One quick look back and he could see the two guys were deciding what to do.

"We were told to stay here," the guy in black said.

"What if it's them? We should open it."

"They would have called us." The guy in black turned back to face Eri and Charlie, just as Teddy ducked behind a post holding a horse blanket.

The banging came again, and then Willow's voice. "Hey, who is in my barn? You don't belong in there. I'm calling the cops." There were footsteps as if she was retreating. *Clever girl.*

"I thought you said they rented this place."

"I thought so, too." The guy in black licked his lips. "Go handle it. We can't have any witnesses. And definitely no cops."

The other guy nodded and exited through the side door. *And then there was one.* Teddy fingered a knife in his belt, lifted it out, aimed, and tossed. It landed at the base of the man's skull. With a slight moan, he folded over onto the floor.

Teddy ran forward and removed the hoods from both of his friends' heads. Their eyes lit up, but their mouths were taped shut with duct tape. "Sorry about this." With one pull, he yanked each off.

"Ouch," Eri said. "No need to get my lip waxed

anytime soon."

"You wax your lip?" Charlie said, with an amused grin.

"Shut up, Charlie." Eri frowned. "All women do eventually."

Teddy cut the plastic bindings from both their hands. "Can you walk? We still have one more bad guy."

"Not anymore," Willow said in his ear. "Target neutralized."

Eri rubbed her hands and paced a few steps. "Does anyone else think this is too simple?"

Charlie nodded. "We weren't the targets. They had a fifty percent chance to get away with Laura and Myers, and they did."

Teddy sighed. "One point them, zip to us."

The three of them walked through the side door and met Willow at the car.

"So, what now, boss?" Teddy asked, looking at Eri.

"Ha, I'm hardly the one in charge. This will be Charlie's big moment." She faced him and grinned. "Break out your equipment, honey. We have some bad guys to fry."

"Yes, ma'am." Charlie climbed in the back and retrieved his laptop. "But I don't think we should stay here. The bad guys could come back, and there are no guarantees the cops won't show, too. Two dead bodies are no good."

"Yeah, let's move. I know a place not far from here." Teddy walked to the driver's side and opened the door. "When I was little, my mom and dad would come visit my uncle on his turkey farm...gross animals, by the way. Nothing worse than turkey poop and the sound of thousands of gobblers at once. Man, I tell you, it made you want to pray for Thanksgiving." He climbed in and joined Charlie. "Not that I don't always love Thanksgiving. Nothing like mashed potatoes and stuffing. My grandma made great stuffing. I especially love the pecans and olives she put in that bird. Not that my uncle ever had us over to kill one of those nasty turkeys, mind you. Just to eat. And the gravy—"

"Teddy?" Charlie said with a bit of annoyance.

"Sorry. Yes. Anyway, his farm is about thirty minutes from here. He would probably let us stay the night. We could get rested and cleaned up, look stuff up, like you do. What do you think?"

"Sounds good." Charlie hit Teddy on the back and smiled at Eri.

Teddy knew he prattled and he always detected the annoyance smile, but he didn't care. It was who he was, and it kept him sane. "Then strap in ya'll, we're going to a turkey farm."

Chapter Twenty-One

Laura must have fallen asleep. When she opened her eyes, there was a soft glow from a single light bulb hanging to her right. She glanced around the space. *Some sort of basement.* Myers lay strapped to a bed, his skin visibly moist, and patches of blood lay under his nostrils. His eyes were closed.

"Myers," she hissed.

No response.

"Myers," she said again.

The door to her left squeaked open, and Helena entered. A weird grin decorated her face. She wore latex gloves and vinyl apron. That meant only one thing—torture. "So, Myers seemed to enjoy his time with Harding, and you're next. Only you get me. You lucky, girl, you."

Flashbacks to when Helena had helped them torture that one security guy in Washington D.C. came into Laura's mind. No doubt now, this woman was well trained—a *bona fide* agent. Never had she been what they thought—a sad daughter mourning her father. "So, I'm guessing you're not Julio's daughter."

"Perceptive."

"So, the losing your dad act was all a ruse."

"Not exactly."

"Why, Helena? Why are you doing this? We were

your family."

"I had a family!" She grabbed Laura up by the hair and tossed her hard onto a metal cot. Something sharp hit Laura's hip, causing it to sting. The chains from the wall pulled at her wrists, drawing her back.

"And I did lose my father. Just not Julio." Helena undid one chain at a time and cuffed Laura's wrists to a metal pole that ran the length of the cot on both sides. "You're so naïve, Black."

"Chappelle."

"Not…any…more," Helena sang.

Laura tried to get up, wanting more than anything to rip that disgusting grin off her face. "What is wrong with you?"

"What is wrong with *me*?" Helena shook her head. "No, it's what is wrong with you. That is the reason we are all here, Agent *Black*. The reason Bryce had to die is on you."

Laura glared at her. "Don't ever say his name again."

"It's the reason Denise had to die." Helena turned her back and zipped open a leather knife case. Ironically, the case had been a gift from Bryce and Laura for Christmas. "It's the reason for everything, really."

Fine, Laura would bite. "What? What is the reason?"

Helena turned around, methodically rocking a four-inch knife hilt in the palm of her other hand. "You don't remember me from before, but I remember you." She circled around the cot. "I was only seventeen. It had been a glorious day. I had just gotten an acceptance to college in the States and couldn't wait to tell my father all about it. I came home super excited, only to find him shot twice…once in the back and once in the head…dead." Helena straddled the cot. "Shot by your hand."

Laura stared at her, unsure how to take this news. In a mere whisper, she asked, "Who was your father?"

"Ignacio Perez." Tears began to well in her eyes. "And you murdered him!" She jammed the knife hard into Laura's left shoulder.

Laura screamed. Pain pierced through her upper body. Blood pooled around the embedded weapon, running down her chest and arm. Once she could focus, she began to remember the name Perez, just not the incident. But the betrayal now had a name, a reason. Helena was trying to avenge her father. It was why she killed Bryce. *To get to me.* Though it didn't change how Laura felt, it did make her understand. "I'm sorry about your dad, Helena. I'm sure I was only following Greenstone's orders."

"You're sure? Like you don't remember?" Helena lifted her leg back to the other side of the cot, toward the table, and reached for another knife. "You don't get to apologize. You just get to suffer like I suffered."

"Helena, please," Myers said, obviously now awake.

Laura turned to face him. His eyes were red and swollen, his face ashen and sweaty. He nodded to the knife still in Laura's shoulder. Knowing him, he was trying to distract Helena so Laura could find a way to palm it.

"Helena, please?" she mocked. "Myers, you're so ridiculous. Who gets married as a teenager anyway? Trust me, I did you and Denise a favor. There was no way that was going to last."

Myers thrashed around like a caged animal, trying to fight against the bindings holding him to the bed.

Laura tried to use her neck to get the knife. It was too far down to reach.

"So, who gets it next?" Helena dug in her pocket and pulled out a coin. "Heads, Laura gets it. Tails, it's all Myers." She flipped the coin and let it fall to the floor.

"Why are you doing this? Doesn't my love for you over the past year count for anything?" Myers tried to reach their captor.

"Heads it is." She grabbed another knife and jammed it toward Laura's left hand.

It slid between Laura's two fingers, missing most of her hand. She winced, but the pain was manageable.

"Aw, better luck next time." Helena pouted. "And there will be a next time." She spun on her heel and faced Myers. "And what love? I went into your home knowing this day would come. It was the only thing that kept me sane."

"Hardly," Laura sneered.

"You deserve this."

"Maybe, but why Myers? I thought you cared about him."

Helena crossed to where he laid and ran a hand over his now bald head. "Oh, I do. But I needed a witness, and he drew the short straw." She leaned over and kissed him hard on the mouth. When she pulled back, Myers spit in her face.

Helena didn't even flinch. A sardonic smile crossed her lips as she slowly raised a hand to wipe off the spittle. "Well, I think that's enough for now. Get your rest, my two friends. You're going to need it." She started to walk out, then turned back. "Oh, what am I thinking? Laura's rule number one, never leave weapons in the vicinity of an agent." With one swift move, Helena yanked both knives out of Laura's body.

Laura screamed. Her head spun, and then everything went black.

****

When she opened her eyes again, Laura sat on the floor, once again chained in the dark next to Myers. Her shoulder throbbed, but it felt bandaged. Why torture her and then treat the wounds? It didn't make sense. "Myers?"

"Yeah, I'm here."

"She treated my wounds."

"Yeah, mine too."

"Why? Doesn't that seem strange?" Laura scooted closer. His arm came around her. "Are your hands untied?"

"I'm in some kind of harness, but my arms are unrestricted."

"Can you do anything to free us?"

"No, I tried. You have a lock on yours and without anything to pick it with—"

Laura smiled. "Then we're in luck, my friend. Under my armpit, I keep a small pin for such an occasion."

Myers laughed. "Of course, you do."

It took some fancy maneuvering, and a dozen angst-filled tries, but they finally managed to get the pin out.

"Whatever you do, do not drop it. This is our one shot."

"Yes, ma'am." Myers chuckled. He went to work on the lock. Luckily, breaking and entering was one of his many skills. Charlie always joked he was better, but Laura knew Myers was the best thief after having witnessed him successfully pick many locks over the last two years. His body pushed into hers, his breath hot on her neck as he tried to free her. The closeness caught her off guard. She hadn't been this close with anyone but Bryce in a long time. Tears trickled down her face.

She didn't know why this moment was overwhelming her. The reality that Bryce and Denise were truly gone hit like a huge weight to her chest. Not really a great time to grieve, but who really gets to choose that? Without warning, sobs wracked her entire body.

Myers stopped and pulled back. "Are you okay?" His tone was soft with concern.

"Remember your moment at the gas station last year?"

"I understand." He pulled her close and held her tight. "Take your time. I'm here."

She nodded, though he could not see her. After a moment, she breathed deep and said, "It's okay. Continue. I'll be fine. I just really needed to get that out."

"Grief is a wily monster and hits at the most inopportune times." A click sounded in the darkness. "But there is a silver lining…" He pulled at the straps, and her wrists were free. "You're the toughest person I know. Ready to get out of here, my dear friend?"

Chapter Twenty-Two

Helena stared at the monitors, yawning. The green hue of the night vision made Laura and Myers ghostly white. Watching them gave her a sense of power, but at the same time, it made prolonging her retribution harder. Suddenly, she realized they were moving away from where they were chained. *Well, that didn't take long.* "Hey, it looks like they're free."

Alicia leaned over her right shoulder and smiled. "Perfect. Now the fun begins. I'll go get Harding."

"Why can't we just shoot her and be done with it?" Annoyed, Helena turned away from the monitors in the rolling chair.

"Because this isn't just about your revenge, or mine. It's bigger than that, and you know it." She spun back and walked toward Helena. "This is about that woman being the bane of not only our existence but a nuisance and a traitor to the S.I.U. Besides, Harding is not even the top dog anymore. I'm not even sure if he's sanctioned to kill her." Alicia patted Helena's arm and walked back to the door. "Which means, we surely aren't."

Helena peered back at the monitor with disgust. Maybe an accident could occur, and Laura would just die. All this torture, as fun as it might be, was getting old. Helena had waited several years to make this day come true, and it could only have one ending—the funeral of Laura Black. *Get on with it already.*

Myers and Laura appeared to be scanning the room. Likely looking for weapons and a way out. Little did they know this ruse was just part of the plan. *They think they are all smart, so why don't they know that?* "Good luck, guys. You're going to need it," Helena mocked.

Harding walked in and nudged her out of the way to get a better view of the monitor. "Have they found the exit yet?"

"No. They just got free from their bindings."

He sat in the chair closest to the keyboard and hit a few buttons to change the camera setting. The two of them stood looking right into the new camera angle. Laura whispered something to Myers. He nodded and then boosted her up on his shoulders. She reached forward, her hand covering the lens, and then the feed turned to static.

"Well, we had to know that would happen," Helena snickered.

"Of course." Harding punched a few more keys, and another view came onto the monitor. "There."

"Out of curiosity," Helena leaned against the counter, "When are we going to kill them?"

Harding clicked a few more buttons, turning on a few more cameras, and responded dryly, "Never."

Fire burned in her chest and cheeks. She stood with crossed arms. "What do you mean never?"

"Never. This is about conditioning them back into good soldiers. Laura was the best to ever serve at S.I.U., and Myers has proven his worth time and time again. So, the plan is to turn them back into loyal agents. I thought you understood that?" Harding turned to stare her in the eye, his tone filled with a strong warning. "No one will be killing them. *You* will not be killing them."

It took every ounce of control for Helena to not scream and punch this guy in the face, to not reach for her gun and shoot this man where he sat. Anger blurred her vision, but using all she had learned here, she worked to control her breathing and any sign of physical emotion. The worst thing she could do was play her hand too early. Letting Harding know how she really felt would only end in her death. It was now evident Laura was his prize, and Helena was merely a puppet to bring her to him. One inclination that she planned to defy him, and Harding would settle it with a bullet to her brain. No hesitation. She had seen it before when someone disobeyed him. No, she would play along—for now. "Of course. What do we do next?"

"Keep watching them. This entire place was rigged by Gael. The man knows his torture. Gotta love him. Sleep deprivation. Hunger. Thirst. Fluctuating temperatures. Lights too bright, lights too dim, annoying sounds…you name it. In one week, they will be begging for us to end their lives. Instead, we will begin to build them back up." Harding hit a key and a thermometer on the screen rose to 100 degrees. "We'll start with making it extremely uncomfortable."

Helena smiled. Though it wasn't her preferred outcome, the continual torture of her enemy would be fun. However, the idea of Laura being her co-agent did not sit well. First chance to kill her in the field, Helena would take it. The only reason she had waited until now is because she always assumed it ended with Laura dying. That hope was now dashed. What she would give to go back to standing over Laura with that knife so long ago. It would have had a different outcome.

Alicia strutted in wearing a tight black dress and knee-high boots—hardly befitting a secret agent on duty. But then, the girl never followed protocol, not even in training. She spit, cussed, hit, and basically, gave every leader in this place a hard time. That was until they locked her in the pit for two weeks. She came out very ill, but with an entirely different attitude.

Harding drew Alicia to him and kissed her passionately on the lips.

Gross. Helena grimaced and turned away. Though he was only a few years older, it looked wrong. It felt wrong. Helena focused on the screen. Myers discovered another hidden camera, and for a moment, it seemed like he was looking at her. Helena's heart leapt. Though she betrayed him, there were real feelings between them. But her hatred for Laura overpowered her love for Myers, and she had made her choice. Deep inside, she wondered if he would ever forgive her? Once he was broken, would he be hers again? She hoped that could happen. Her heart ached to hold him, to kiss him, to love him again.

His hand came near the lens and technical snow filled the screen.

"He found another camera."

Harding turned from the lust in his arms and leaned to the monitor. He smelled like cigarettes and coffee. *How could Alicia kiss that? Once again, gross.* Harding clicked a few more keystrokes, and a bird's eye view filled the screen. Brilliant. A camera in the ceiling. "How many of those do you have?"

"Enough." He slapped her shoulder and turned back to Alicia. "I have to attend a meeting. Keep an eye on things, will you?"

"You bet. See you tonight." Alicia winked.

Shaking her head, Helena turned back to the screen just in time to see Laura disappear into the ceiling. "She's in the ducts."

Alicia slipped into the chair next to hers. "We'll see which ways she goes. Hot or cold?"

"Did you know all along Harding didn't plan to kill her?"

Alicia shrugged. "I suppose. I know she's his pet."

"And that doesn't bother you? I mean, you are dating the man."

She traced the inside of her lips with her long fingernail and smiled. "We aren't dating. That isn't what this is."

"Just answer the question."

"I guess."

"And that doesn't bother you?"

"Whatever happens, happens."

Helena faced Alicia and stared at the girl she had spent the last few years getting to know. S.I.U. made them eat together, bunk together, basically do everything that didn't include a toilet break together, for over a year. When they went into the field, they wanted the two of them to pass as sisters. That could only happen if they were super close to one another. It had worked. They bonded. But now, it was like that other girl didn't exist. Never her true friend. Just passing time to be placed on the case. Who knew? "What has happened to you?"

"Nothing." She shrugged. "I don't know what you

mean."

"Nothing? When you and I first met, you were just as angry as me." Helena could not believe how passive she was being. Incensed, she slid back in the chair and stood, pointing, her hand shaking. "She killed not only your father, but your entire family with that bomb. Do you not remember? Don't you care anymore?" She shook her head and mocked, "Whatever happens, happens?"

Alicia folded her fist under her chin and leaned forward on the desk. "She didn't kill my family."

Helena faced her, legs apart, arms folded. "What?"

Alicia yawned before tucking a strand of hair behind her ear with a manicured nail. A small sardonic grin passed over her features. "This was never about us, but always about you. We knew if we fed that rage, you'd do the right thing. So, he put me in as your handler. The only way it worked is if I could identify with you."

Helena could not fully comprehend what she was hearing. Was she merely a pawn to bring Laura in? Her legs wobbled. She stepped back and sat in a chair by the door.

Alicia didn't seem to care she had just dropped a bomb; she just went back to the monitors.

"Did you ever care about me?" Helena squeaked.

"Sure." Alicia glanced over her shoulder. "About as much as you cared about Laura's team."

Tears welled in Helena's eyes. Why did that bother her so much? Probably because she felt betrayed and realized she didn't have one friend in the world. The ones she had, she betrayed, and the one she thought she still had betrayed her. This was getting worse.

Chapter Twenty-Three

Laura wedged her legs between the two panels of the ceiling duct and put her hands down to Myers. The man was a brute, pulling him up would not be easy.

"Just pull to get my hands on the opening, and I can lift my own body weight," he said.

She complied. Within seconds, Myers was in the space, too. Sweat beaded her face and body. Turning the heat up was a sure sign this was about conditioning. This wasn't her first rodeo. She knew this company inside and out. They didn't plan to kill her, but rather reprogram her.

Often, it worked. She had seen rebellious teens turn into robots after conditioning exercises. But she was Laura Black-Chappelle. No way could S.I.U. have her again. She crawled down the duct until it hit an end and then kicked out the vent and dropped to what looked like a boiler room.

Myers joined her.

She leaned to his ear, "You cannot let them have you. No matter what they do to us. Understand?"

He pulled back and met her stare. "There is nothing they could do to turn me. No matter what, I'm with you, Charlie, and Eri. I trust only them, and my loyalty is always to you guys." He touched her stomach. "And to him or her."

That surprised her, but she let it go. "Helena is here. It may come down to you choosing to shoot her or join her."

There was conflict in his expression. She knew it. Could he pull the trigger and kill the woman he started to love? Flashes of Bryce filled Laura's mind. If the roles were reversed, there was no way she could have ever killed him. Love fell deep. It got in crevices nothing else could inhabit.

With a hardened stare, Myers clenched his jaws and answered, "She killed Denise. That cancels all of it. Any love that was there is now replaced with disgust. The woman I thought I loved did not even exist."

Laura wrapped her arms around Myers' torso. He was too tall for her to reach his neck. He touched her back. Together, they would get through this. Somehow, she had developed a real bond with Myers lately. Her heart softened in his hug. Whatever it took, she would get them out of here—alive—and back with their family. "Let's go."

The boiler room was even hotter than where they had been before. Loud engines turned and heat radiated off them making the room almost unbearable. Sweat damped their hair and clothing. Together, they walked around in circles for close to an hour, finding no exit. Nothing but the vent they had entered.

"What now?" Myers yelled loud enough for her to hear it over the machines.

Laura usually had the answer, but not today. "I don't know much, but I know we cannot stay in here. We'll die."

"Do these machines have water?"

"If they do, it would be boiling." Laura glanced at

the vent. "We need to go back up there and see where else it might take us."

Myers sauntered to bottom of the vent. "Let me go first though. I can pick you up easier."

Laura nodded and then cupped her hand to give him a boost. He stepped in and jumped to the opening. His muscles had to be screaming. In this heat, with no water, they had little energy left. He reached down from the hole. Laura had to leap three times, but finally made it. They crawled in silence back to the space they had come from. Before dropping back in their locked room, Laura wanted to see if there was anything the other way. She crawled over the hole and started down the other path. The comforting sense of cool temperatures began to flow through the space. The closer she got to the end, the cooler it got. She kicked out the grate and jumped down. Relief filled her body. *A walk-in cooler.* The wet clothes and sweat on her body made her cold, and instantly, she was freezing.

Myers jumped down, closed his eyes, and breathed deep. "Now this is what I am talking about."

Laura went to the handle on the freezer. It wouldn't budge. She tried again. No luck. "Myers?"

Myers walked to the handle and tried it. It didn't move.

"We need to go back. I don't know how long we can survive in here."

He nodded and walked back to the hole.

Suddenly, a metal door shifted over the hole above.

Panic shot through Laura's heart. "No!"

Myers cupped his hands. "Jump up and see."

Laura stepped in and leapt at the metal door. Hard, stiff, not going to budge. "We're trapped." She stepped back down, rubbing her arms. "I didn't think they wanted to kill us. I figured it was torture, or conditioning, but not this."

"Maybe it still is. How long can we last in here?"

"Maybe fifteen to twenty minutes."

"Body heat," Myers said, teeth chattering. "We need to remove our wet clothes."

There were bags of potatoes wrapped in burlap to her left. "Yeah, I have another idea too."

He saw the point of her gaze and must have read her mind. They quickly dumped the potatoes from the sacks and then popped holes through the bottom. Myers pulled off his black shirt. His muscles were dotted with goose bumps. He turned away while Laura pulled off her T-shirt. Both wrapped in the scratchy cloths.

Myers shifted to the corner of the room filled with cardboard boxes of vegetables that would hopefully give them more insulation. He sat with his knees bent and spread apart. Laura wedged between them as he wrapped his arms around her arms. They weren't warm, but they helped. Within seconds, her body temperature raised some.

"I'm sorry this is happening to you," Myers whispered in her ear.

She shook her head. "I'm sorry this is happening to us."

He held her tight, rubbing her arms periodically.

Her mind began to soften and sleep threatened to take her. She closed her eyes.

Myers jolted her awake with hard shake. "Don't fall asleep, Laura. You know this."

That would not be easy. "I don't think we're going to make it."

"I thought you said they didn't want to kill us."

What did she know? Greenstone was dead, and Harding had his own ways of doing things. "I have no idea anymore."

"Do you think they are watching?"

Laura glanced around the cooler. A small camera lay just above the shelf. "I know they are." She pulled a hand out from under the burlap and waved at the camera. "They wouldn't miss this show for anything."

Suddenly, the lock on the freezer door clicked.

Both jumped up. Stars threatened to drop her, but Laura blinked to stay conscious. She tried the handle. It opened. Both rushed through and into a kitchen. Without hesitation, Laura ran to the water faucet and began drinking. Myers joined her. Once she had some water in her system, she turned for the drawers and started searching for a weapon. She had opened the second drawer when a group of agents with guns loped in. The men surrounded them and waited without a word. Normally, Laura would have tried to take them all out, but right now, she was too lethargic to do anything. A Hispanic man waved his gun at both of them, and said, "Let's go."

Myers handed Laura her T-shirt. She dropped the potato sack and struggled to pull it on over her head. Together, they pushed past the armed men, walking back to their room. Inside, Helena stood with a scowl and a syringe. "On your knees, now!"

Laura glanced at Myers. His lips were tight, his face taught like stone. Hatred poured from his eyes. She could only imagine the betrayal he felt. After Denise, it took everything in him to love again, and it was nothing more than deception.

Defiantly, Myers crossed his arms and spread his legs shoulder width apart. Obviously, he was not going down by his own will.

Laura decided to be more compliant. Right now, she wanted the nap guaranteed in that syringe. Her body felt like gelatin, and her head was pounding with pain. She kneeled to the floor and bent her head to the side, revealing an open neck.

"How submissive of you."

"Helena, you can't keep drugging her. There's something you should know."

"Myers, don't."

Helena walked in front of her, pulled her hair before jamming the needle deep into Laura's skin. "Watch me."

She winced. Then darkness.

Chapter Twenty-Four

Teddy knocked back two aspirins, trying to block out the incessant gobbling of their feathered cover. Protection or not, hundreds of turkeys gobbling were going to drive them insane. "I think I'd rather face Harding's goons."

"How long do we have to stay here again?" Eri asked with her elbows covering her ears.

"I think we should find another place to stay, man." Charlie clicked a few buttons on the laptop and spun it around. "There is a bed and breakfast about a mile from here. We could pretend to be two couples in from the trails."

Teddy's heart flipped. Would he and Willow have to share a room? Not that he minded, but he was still trying to believe that kiss was actually real. "Sure." His voice cracked, and he cleared it. "Sure, sounds good. Anything is better than here."

Willow nodded from behind a bandana she had wrapped around her face to block out the smell.

"Good, it's settled. Let's go." Charlie led them back to the green car and jumped in the driver's seat with Eri next to him.

Willow and Teddy piled in back. The drive wasn't long, but there was definitely heated tension between the two of them. Was she worried about staying in the same room, too? Did she want to? Did he want to? Even though they sat a few inches away from each other, it was as if they were holding each other passionately. She glanced his way and smiled coyly. He grinned back. Like a game of checkers, each took his or her turn looking, flirting, smiling, and sending awkward messages with their eyes. Not one sound, yet volumes of story were written in those few miles. He swallowed.

When the car parked, both jumped out.

Charlie and Eri were oblivious. The two of them were married. What did they have to worry about? Teddy had only had one other sort-of girlfriend in his life—Alicia. And that was extremely short lived and barely counted. Truth be told, he was hardly a ladies' man. Women made him nervous. Most of his incessant talking was due to his nervousness around them. In this moment, he felt very uncomfortable but also excited at the expectation of spending some time with Willow alone.

Which was it? He had no idea. Like everything else in his life, he'd play it by ear. They could always keep one foot on the floor like the old days. But wouldn't she find that weird. Most women did. Why would she be any different? Could he even act normal with her in the same room? Of course, they had been alone before at the house. Why was this different? Nothing would happen. *Stop torturing yourself, Teddy. This is stupid.*

He grabbed his duffle bag and scuffled behind the group, silent, which was probably a dead giveaway that something was up. He always talked. Never quiet. They would know. *She* would know. Panic enveloped him. Perspiration soaked his beanie. Was this really happening? Was he about to share a room with the beautiful Willow? What then? Was it even kosher? Call him a prude, but he came from a very conservative background. His mother would kill him if she didn't think he was already dead.

Charlie held the door open for all of them and then walked around to the desk. "Hello, we would like to get two rooms. We just had a long day and need to stay for just one night. We don't believe much in technology, so I hope cash will be okay."

Teddy tried not to laugh. He was surprised the "king of technology" could even get that sentence out with a straight face.

"Cash will be fine as long as there is no hanky panky going on here." The older woman glanced at both girls. They both smiled, and the lady narrowed her eyes, and then nodded. "Okay." She spun a book around and pointed. "Sign here."

"No, ma'am. No hanky panky. This is my wife and her sister."

The woman raised an eyebrow. After all, Eri was Chinese and Willow was a pale redhead. "And the young man?"

"Long-lost cousin. He can stay with me." Charlie wrapped his arm around Teddy. "The girls can have the other room."

Teddy didn't know if he was relieved or sad. On one hand, the stress of what to do about Willow was gone. On the other hand, a small part of him wanted to spend time with her, discuss that kiss. But this was better. He was slightly sure.

The two of them split ways in the hall. Charlie opened the door to a room filled with antique furniture that smelled of mothballs and wood oil. The bed was swathed in a quilted cover and looked to only be a full size. "Well, this will be cozy."

Charlie laughed. "It's fine. You can have it. I can sleep on the floor."

"Are you sure?"

"Dude, I'm so exhausted from the drugs and all that happened to us today, trust me, I could sleep anywhere." He grabbed one of the extra pillows from the back of the bed, tossed it on the floor, and then grabbed a comforter from a rocking chair. "Night."

"Night."

Teddy turned a key on the side of the lamp and the room fell dark. He pulled off his hoodie and shoes and climbed between the blankets and sheet. It was cool and comfortable, but every time he turned, the bed squeaked, waking him again.

Charlie obviously didn't notice. He was out, snoring.

Too many memories and ideas flashed through Teddy's mind. He tried to clear it, but he worried about his friends and what was to become of them. So much had happened in the last week. More bad than good. Usually, he was the optimistic one. But right now, he was overwhelmed with sadness, as well as, anger.

How could Charlie, or any of them, sleep right now? He rolled out of the bed, trying not to step on Charlie as he exited the room. The hall was eerily quiet, but every step on the old wood planked floor groaned in complaint. Wincing with each step, he tipped toed down the staircase and out onto the veranda. The breeze felt soft to his skin. He inhaled deep and closed his eyes.

"Couldn't sleep either, huh?"

He turned around to see Willow wrapped in a blanket sitting on a porch swing, smiling. "No, and to be honest, I don't know how anyone can."

"Eri said they were drugged with something, and it hadn't worn off yet. She was pretty much out the second she laid down."

"Yeah, Charlie too." Teddy pointed to the swing. "May I?"

She unfolded her legs and patted the seat. "Please."

He sat next to her and sighed. "I just want Laura and Myers to be okay. To find Deshawn. We have no leads, and to be honest, I'm worried."

"Me too." Willow scooted over and laid her head against his arm. "We've seen what they can do. And I'm still trying to wrap my head around Helena killing Bryce. How is that even possible? We all loved him. It's just vile."

"Yeah, I know."

The two of them sat in silence, mourning the death of one friend and the loss of three more. It was too much pain for any person to endure, especially in such a short amount of time. Silently, Teddy prayed for their safety. He couldn't lose anyone else. Laura was like a big sister. Though Myers teased Teddy, he always had his back. Looking high up into the star-filled sky, Teddy whispered, "Please God, watch over our friends."

"Amen," Willow's hushed tone answered. They sat there for a while in silence, and then she broke it. "Can I ask you a question?"

"Of course, anything." He thought about that. "Well, almost anything. Nothing about my childhood. Super embarrassing. I was quite the nerd. I know, hard to believe, but so true."

She touched her lips to his and smiled. "You're babbling."

"Sorry, I do that when I'm nervous, and I guarantee that doesn't help."

"I've noticed."

"What did you want to ask me?"

"Will you be my boyfriend?"

A loud laugh escaped his mouth before he could stop it.

She frowned.

"Sorry, that was... I didn't mean, yes, I would love that."

A grin replaced her frown. "I know that is way more formal than most people today get, but hey, we're still young. We should act young sometimes."

"I agree wholeheartedly." He wrapped his arm around her and pulled her close.

"So why don't you want to share your childhood story. You know my awful tale," Willow said. "How did you end up in Harding's clutches?"

"Sad story actually. My mom passed away. My dad stopped working. We couldn't pay the rent, and I ended up on the street. I began hanging out with dog fighters."

"Dog fighters?"

"People who fight for money. Sometimes with real dogs. Sometimes people against people."

"Awe, go on."

"Well, I started fighting just to eat. One day, one of Harding's men was there recruiting. Saw me and promised me a better life."

"And you took it?"

He shrugged. "I was hungry."

"Yeah, I guess I get that." She turned her face up to see his. "Would you still do it knowing what you know now? Ending with these people?"

"Knowing I'd be with you?" He kissed her softly on the nose. "It is possible."

She pushed into his shoulder and closed her eyes. Soon, he did the same and drifted off to sleep.

Chapter Twenty-Five

Helena stared at the monitor with clenched teeth. After over an hour of torture, Laura now lay with her head in Myers' lap. Gently, he stroked her hair, whispering non-discernable words in her ear. "Why must we let them stay together? It doesn't make sense." Helena turned from the monitors and glared at Harding. "Wouldn't it make more sense and be much better in the long run to keep those two apart?"

"No, it wouldn't. Though I do not owe you an explanation, I need them thinking as a single unit. Either they are both broken together or one will always rebel and try to free the other. And I can't have that, now can I?" Harding nudged her from the chair. "Your feelings for this man are distracting, and honestly, super annoying."

His gaze hardened. A vein pulsated on his forehead as his eyes narrowed. "I hope you haven't forgotten the stakes here. This is not about you at all. Nothing here has anything to do with you. Myers will never be yours, even if he turns. Remember there is no fraternization in S.I.U., so get your mind right, or you'll be joining them down there, chained to a wall. Do I make myself coherent in that insignificant brain of yours?"

Queasiness swept through Helena's stomach. She felt ill. This mission continued to get worse. She had no delusions of regaining Myers' trust, but maybe, somewhere in the recesses of her mind, she hoped.

Alicia pranced in wearing a low-cut top and tight, black jeans. She wrapped her arms around Harding's shoulders and leaned to whisper something in his ear. A seductive smile played on his lips as he whispered something back.

"No fraternization, right," Helena mumbled under her breath, moving toward the door. "I'm taking my break."

They didn't seem to hear her as she left. But who cares? Over all the years she had been with S.I.U., not once did any of the leaders appreciate her devotion or her sacrifice to the so-called cause. She gave this place more than just her physical being—every ounce of who she was seeped into this life. All the decisions and lies, they were all for what she saw as the perfect retribution.

Without any complaint, she buddied up to her father's assassin. For what? To find out they weren't even going to kill her? And to find out her friendship and entire cause with Alicia was just one big lie. That she would never experience love again. How much more could Helena take? Not that it mattered. Life with S.I.U. was "until death do we part"—a true marriage. It was no wonder the *Black Squad* chose to flee from this place two years ago.

Helena sighed as she neared the end of the hallway and pushed open the control room door. How stupid were Laura and Bryce back then to think they could escape all of this? There was no escaping the S.I.U.— not really. Everyone knew this organization would always come for their people, as was evidenced by the blood trickling from Black's and Myers' bodies onto the cement floor downstairs. If they couldn't break them, they would kill them.

The long, dim hallway from the control room seemed to go on forever. This place was crazy hot. Sweat poured down her face and back as she reached the end by the boiler room. She lifted a small plate revealing a light panel and punched in the code. The wall slid to the right, exposing a service elevator.

She stepped inside and inhaled the cool rush of air, before punching the fourth floor button. The door closed, and the elevator rose. It stopped short and opened, revealing she was home. The hallway was flooded with teenagers gabbing about stupid stuff, messing around. Some were flirting, others studying. If someone didn't know any better, it could be any college dorm or military barracks.

"Helena?" someone said behind her.

She spun around, coming face to face with Deshawn. Her heart skipped. She was the one who knocked him out in Mexico and saw when Alicia and another man took him. But she assumed he was dead. "Deshawn, you're here. Why? I mean… What are you doing here?"

"Good to see you, too," he said sarcastically with a raised eyebrow "Of course, I could ask you the same question."

"Right. Of course. Good to see you, man. I was just surprised. That's all." Helena gave him an awkward smile, then glanced around the hallway, before stepping closer so no one could hear them. "I meant, why aren't you with Black's team anymore? What happened? How did you end up here?"

"Someone, I'm assuming an S.I.U. agent, grabbed

me in Mexico, and brought me back here. I don't know why I'm not locked up." He scratched a small goatee forming on his chin. "Did the same happen to you?"

"Not exactly." Helena leaned to one hip and crossed her arms. "I'll admit, I don't quite understand why you aren't locked up either. After all, you're good friends with the enemy."

He looked at her sideways, obviously confused. "Aren't you?"

Did she tell him the truth? A part of her wanted to tell him everything. To somehow gain his trust and have a friend again. But that isn't what would happen. She knew it. It was better she got him in line with the program. "It's important to know who the real enemy is, Deshawn." She glanced up at a camera and made sure he saw it, too. "S.I.U. is your family now. Don't forget that."

He opened his mouth to speak, but she didn't wait for him to express his thoughts. Nothing he said would make her feel good. Besides, it was time to sleep. After over twenty hours awake, her bunk called her name.

At the end of the hall, she slid her barrack's access open. When she turned to shut it, she noticed Deshawn standing outside the open doorway. She stared at him a moment, then closed the door without a word. He would not be easy to shake. Maybe she should speak to Harding about rethinking his decision to not lock him up. Once Deshawn realized her betrayal, he could become a huge problem. And worse, if he got wind of their captives in the basement, he would likely side with Laura and Myers. It was no secret Myers and he were good friends.

Sitting on a chair next to the small desk in her

room, Helena unlaced her boots. Why was Harding keeping him out in the open? None of this made sense to her. In one swift motion, she tossed her body on the bunk and stared at the ceiling. Smoke rings stained the ceiling from years of smokers using this room. Supposedly, this station was the first S.I.U. outpost. Most thought S.I.U. started in Puerto Rico, but actually, it began on the border of El Paso, Texas and Mexico. It made it easy for Greenstone to get away with stuff, without having to travel so far from the U.S.

Her mind whirled with all that had happened lately. Harsh thoughts about Harding's behavior drifted through her memory. She worked to piece all the weird decisions together. He had said something about wanting Laura and Myers to be broken *together*. Some of it started to make more sense. He was right. If one of them were still against S.I.U., they would be a hindrance to the other. Maybe Deshawn was there to remind them of what they had before and to make this place home again. Or maybe Harding wanted him to know about them and test his loyalty. If he failed, he would die as an example. One more nail to Laura's psyche.

Deshawn may try to help Laura escape, but then, he would be where they were. If he passed and they were assimilated back into this place, then they would be a strong unit. But Helena didn't want that. She wanted them all to fail. Better yet, she yearned for Laura to die trying to escape. Deshawn was just one more distraction to Helena's end game. He had to go as soon as possible.

She rolled over on her bunk and squeezed her eyes shut. Visions of Myers holding her, caressing her, kissing her beset her mind. A part of those gave her warmth. But they were quickly replaced with how he would speak to her now. The few words they had exchanged had been bitter, full of disgust and fury. He would never forgive her, and if he did by some chance, there was no fraternization at S.I.U.

Her heart hurt. She needed to find peace, but that was long ago taken by Laura's hand. All of this was her fault. All of it. A new rage flooded Helena's system. She swung her legs to the floor and hopped up. She dropped to the floor and began pressing out push-ups. Every fiber of her body tingled with rile. She had to find a way to kill Laura that wouldn't get her killed. Maybe then, and only then, would Helena finally find peace.

Chapter Twenty-Six

Teddy slowly opened his eyes, unsure of where he was. Stiff pain clenched his neck as he labored to sit up. Willow lay next to him on the swing, her head resting on his thigh. In the distance, rays of purple and orange rose over a clump of trees. Birds chirped announcing the new day. Yawning, Teddy stretched in some effort to clear his aching muscles.

"Good morning," Willow croaked next to him. "How did you sleep?"

He glanced at her and smiled. "Good morning. As well as to be expected on a porch swing. You?"

"Same," she giggled. Slowly, she slid up and away from him. Marks from the fabric of his sweats lined her face, but even then, she was beautiful. "To be honest, I can't believe we fell asleep out here."

"I don't even remember falling asleep."

Willow smiled. "You were telling me some story about a yeti. When I asked you what a yeti was, you started to make fun of me, then mumbled something incoherent. I believe that was when I lost you."

"A yeti is a hairy creature that lives in the Himalayas."

She giggled. "But it's mythical, right?"

"Some would say about as mythical as the Loch Ness Monster."

"Which is also mythical?"

Teddy raised an eyebrow. "What, you don't believe in him? There are real pictures. Real sightings of both."

A cute, amused smile formed on her lips. He started to lean forward, when the screen door creaked open and Charlie peeked around. "Good morning, you two. You guys are up early."

"Had to escape the snoring," Teddy joked.

Charlie turned a cup of coffee in his hand and took a sip before replying, "Be glad Myers isn't here. That boy could snore the rafters off a barn."

"True that." Teddy laughed.

The elderly host poked her head around Charlie. "Breakfast is on the table. Help yourself, dears."

The three nodded and followed her in.

"Where is Eri?" Teddy asked as he sat at the dining room table filled with orange juice, soft buttermilk biscuits, sausage gravy, scrambled eggs, crispy bacon, and a watermelon salad.

"I assume she is still sleeping." Willow asked, walking toward the staircase. "Should I wake her?"

"Nah." Charlie popped a piece of bacon in his mouth. "She isn't much of a breakfast person anyway. We can let her sleep some more. I'll take her a plate of fruit and biscuits when we're done."

As they each filled their plates, a sense of nostalgia rushed through Teddy's being. He tried to remember the last time he had this kind of meal. His grandmother was from Oklahoma and often made breakfast for him growing up. It felt so comforting.

He missed that. He missed her. "Man, this takes me back to old times. Do you ever think about those we left behind?"

Charlie and Willow looked up simultaneously mid-bite.

"I try not to." Willow picked up her napkin and dabbed the corners of her mouth. "It hurts too much."

Charlie shrugged. "I didn't leave much back there, really."

"Yeah, in all honesty, neither did I." Willow reached for the jam. "That's why we were all targets."

"I have some good memories," Teddy said.

Eri walked in, kissed Charlie's head, and slid into the empty chair. "No one woke me."

Willow pointed at Charlie. "He said to let you sleep."

Eri looked at her husband sideways. "He did, did he?"

"As far as missing those from our past, what I have here is much more important." Charlie kissed her hand and their eyes locked. There was no doubt the love they shared. "How did you sleep?"

"Dead to the world." Eri reached for a biscuit and tore it open. "You?"

"Same."

Eri slathered some butter on her biscuit and then said, "It's so peaceful here. I think our next home needs to be some place like this. Quiet with trees, and honestly, I like the birds a lot. So peaceful."

"There are many backyard birds that make those sort of noises. Doves are the ones who *coo*. The rattling noise is likely a ruby-throated hummingbird." Teddy glanced out the screen door. "And the whistle is probably a blue jay, or it could be a meadowlark, though they tend to have pretty territorial sounds."

"That's kind of fascinating." Willow grinned.

"How do you know so much about birds?"

"How do I know much about anything? I read *a lot.*" He wiped a corner of a biscuit across the plate to get the last drop of gravy. "And I try to listen when people say interesting things. It is a great way of absorbing strange facts. Well, that and hours of watching the nature channel."

"What about the melodious sound?" Willow asked.

Teddy listened for a moment. "I think that's a robin."

"Fascinating."

Charlie slid back from the table with his plate in hand. "As soon as we finish up, we need to find a web café or something. There doesn't seem to be any Internet connection here."

The host must have overheard them and entered. "You should be able to find one in Vinton. It's just about thirty miles east."

"Thanks." Charlie smiled and turned to them. "Let's get ready and go."

Once showered with new clothes, the group piled in the car. Willow started closing the passenger door, when out of nowhere shots pelted the side of the car. Everyone ducked down. Hunched as low as he could go, Teddy placed the car in reverse, slammed the gas, and spun the wheel. The vehicle squealed around in a donut shooting rocks out from the tires. He jammed it in drive and pushed the accelerator, rocking them forward. More bullets ricocheted off the back and the window. Glass splintered across the back seat. Eri screamed.

"You okay, Eri?" Charlie asked.

"Yeah, you?"

"Yeah, good. Just get me a gun!"

Eri tossed him an M-16, just as a pair of motorcycles came into view. Charlie twisted in his seat with the rifle in his hand and began shooting semi-automatic bursts.

Eri reached for two handguns under the seat and followed suit.

Shared blasts echoed in the sky. Teddy could only watch from the rearview mirror as he tried to outrun the two bad guys. "Suggestions?"

"Where did they come from?" Willow asked from behind the passenger seat.

"Not important right now. I need to know where to go," Teddy shouted.

Charlie pointed to a freeway ramp just ahead. "There!"

"Are you sure? Freeways can be slow and insane."

"Not sure, but it's our only real choice." Charlie slammed a new magazine in his weapon and twisted around in his seat to fire.

Teddy turned for the interstate. A bullet whizzed by his head, just missing his left ear, landing in the front windshield. One motorcycle accelerated and came on Willow's side.

"Gun," Willow yelled.

Eri tossed one of the Glocks her way.

"Ready?" Teddy asked.

Willow nodded.

Teddy slid the window down.

Willow fired, dropping the man from his bike. The bike traveled with them for a few feet, before toppling over and down the embankment. The other bike drove to the driver's side and fired at Teddy. One bullet caught him in the left wrist. Sharp pain and then numbness, as it went straight through. Blood dripped in his lap. He blinked to stay conscious, but his head spun. The car swerved.

"Teddy!"

"The wheel," he managed to mumble.

Willow grabbed the steering wheel and turned it hard into the motorcycle. It knocked him back and down a side hill. She straightened it and moved to sit on Teddy's lap. He tried to stay conscious. Stars began to filter through his line of sight. "Move over, Teddy."

He slid the best he could over the middle thing. Why couldn't he remember what it was called? Was it a console? He shook his head against the dizziness. Eri leaned over and wrapped a scarf around his wrist. He winced.

"We have to get him to a hospital now," Eri said. "He's losing a lot of blood."

Teddy didn't know what else they said. He only knew he felt cold and wanted to sleep.

Chapter Twenty-Seven

Myers's arms hung above his head in chains. His entire body trembled. The guy named Gael hit him with another jolt of electricity. Every vein tingled in resistance. How much more of this could he take? Time seemed irrelevant in this place, but gauging on how many times they had come to torture them, it had to have been a month or so by now.

The door opened, and Harding entered with his usual cocky smile and sauntered next to the cot. "How are we doing today?"

"I think he's done." He nodded to Laura laid out, chained to the bunk. "Do we want to start on her now?"

"That would probably be good."

Fear gripped Myers' chest. "You can't!"

"What?" Harding circled him and stopped eye to eye with Myers, his breath foul from cigarettes and coffee. "And why is that?"

"Because…"

Harding stared at him for a long time without responding, then stood, and said to the man of torture, "Make her time worse."

"She's pregnant," Myers spat out.

All color seemed to drain from Harding's face. He spun on his heel to face Laura. "Is that true?"

She didn't answer.

Myers mouthed behind her, "I'm sorry."

She shook her head and looked at Harding.

Harding rushed to a box on the counter and began rummaging through it. He withdrew a single syringe and then a plastic band. He tied the plastic band like a tourniquet on Laura's upper right arm and then forced the needle into her skin looking for a vein. Laura grimaced. He pulled it out and pushed it in several times before blood began to flow into the vial. Once it was full, he snapped off the band and started walking to the exit with the sample. He stopped and said without turning, "Put an IV in her arm. She's extremely dehydrated. I could barely find a vein."

"Yes, sir. And the man?"

"Yeah, him too."

Harding exited, and the man complied. He placed Myers on the bed next to Laura, and within moments, both were enjoying an infusion of fluid replacement.

That revitalized Myers to a place he had not been in a long time. Energy surged through his body, and for the first time in over a month, his mind seemed to clear from the haze. They had to get out of here. This gift may not come again. Myers peered around, taking in the situation. What did they have? How far was everything? How could he remove these cuffs? His renewed mind felt busy.

After the IV bags were empty, Gael moved Laura and Myers back to the chained wall. Laura rested her head in Myers' lap. Together, they tried to find comfort in the horrible situation. His head throbbed, and his muscles burned from an hour of electro-shock and extreme beatings. Laura didn't look much better. Caked blood lined her temples and upper lip from Helena's pent-up rage earlier that day. Myers did his best to clean Laura up, but he wasn't doing much better.

"Why did you tell him? They've been torturing me."

Myers turned his head to see her face. "The needles in your hands and stuff, that won't hurt the baby. But electro shock? No way."

"Thank you. You're always there for me." Laura's soft voice soothed him as she reminded him of better times.

"Maybe not always. Do you remember the very first thing I said to you?" Myers asked.

"Of course." Laura grinned. "You called me beautiful, and I said you would refer to me as Agent Black or not at all."

He laughed. "And then I called you—"

"Sweetheart," they said in unison.

"And I dropped you in one motion." She started to laugh, then winced. "It hurts to laugh."

"You okay?"

"I'll live."

"Well, it wouldn't be the first time you'd drop me." He lightly tucked a strand of hair away from her face behind her ear. "You've kind of mastered us all. I'm looking forward to the day when one of us bests you."

"Ha! Good luck."

He smiled. She was probably right. There was a reason she was the best and Harding wanted her back. "Do you remember the time when I started to run, and you tried to shoot me in the head?"

Laura twisted around so he could see her face. "I did not try to shoot you. I hit the branch on purpose. If I wanted to shoot you, I would not have missed. You know this all too well."

The two exchanged a smile. It was sweet, and then it wasn't. Tears filled both of their eyes. Their loss was greater than anything else.

"I'm sorry about everything." Laura turned away and sighed. "I always have this amazing sense of guilt about breaking all of you out. In the past, Bryce would always say, 'Well, then we still wouldn't be free.'"

"Yeah, and he was right."

"Was he really?" Laura moaned as she tried to sit up and face him. "I mean, are we free? Were we ever?"

"We will be." Myers grabbed his stomach as he tried to sit up. His muscles rebelled in pain.

"No, that is probably not true. They will keep us here until we are the murderous zombies they desire." She sighed. "At least if I hadn't broken you all out, Denise and Bryce would still be alive."

"Maybe they'd be alive, but you know the rest of that isn't true. We were a stubborn bunch. With or without you, we were going." Myers glanced around and then leaned into her ear. "Since that juice boost, I feel one-hundred percent better. We need to get out of here. You and I are fighters, not guinea pigs. So, let's stop feeling sorry for ourselves and do whatever it takes to escape. Deal?"

Laura kissed his cheek and nodded with a huge grin. "I knew I liked you, Myers. Deal."

"I think I may have an idea," he whispered.

"I'm game, what?"

A sheepish smile spread across his face. "Don't think I'm weird, but what is the one thing that would send Helena over the edge?"

Laura thought about that for a moment and knew.

"You and me."

"Precisely. From what you've told me a million times, they do not allow fraternization in S.I.U., correct?"

"Correct."

"When they first brought us here, they thought I was conked out, but I wasn't. I overheard Alicia promise Helena she could have me when this was over if she played her cards right."

"Harding would never allow that."

"Yeah, well, that may be true, but what that told me was Helena still has feelings for me."

Laura raised an eyebrow. "Do you for her?"

He grimaced. "Girl, please. I love her about as much as I love a hangover. It was fun while it lasted, and now I am just sick."

Laura laughed. "So, you think if we ham up a relationship, she'll what?"

"She'll make a mistake."

Chapter Twenty-Eight

Laura considered the idea of pretending to like Myers. There was truth to that logic, but it also could mean Laura's early demise. "If we're wrong, I'm dead."

"Right."

"What if you play to her? Try to get her back."

He grimaced.

"I know you hate her, but once it's over, you can pull the trigger."

For a moment, he seemed to ponder that. "I still think—"

The bolt on the door thumped.

Myers grabbed Laura and touched his lips to hers. Passionately, he kissed her. Every muscle in her body tingled. Heat rose down her spine and into her toes. Laura didn't know what surprised her more—that he did it, or that she enjoyed it.

Helena cleared her throat.

Myers withdrew slowly. His eyes spoke volumes of surprise as well. They had endured much together over the last month, but this was unexpected. He was like family. Like a brother. How could there be real attraction?

Helena said something behind them, but it sounded muffled through the nonverbal conversation that occurred between her and Myers. His eyes asked, "Are we okay? Was that bad? Was it the right move?"

Laura nodded. They were okay; it wasn't bad, just confusing.

Helena undid Laura's chain, then yanked her from the ground, and tossed her to the cot. "Harding said you get a time out today, but I disagree." She started to grab the bindings on the side of the cot to secure her, when Laura kicked her in the face. That dropped her to the floor.

Helena stood back up and went for a syringe.

Laura blocked her and shoved her hard into Myers. Myers wrapped chain around Helena's neck. Laura ran for the syringe and pushed it deep into Helena's neck. Within seconds, her body fell limp.

"See, mistake. I knew that would make her be stupid."

Laura grinned. "Yes, I see. But you know they are likely watching. We have to go."

"No, chain her first." Myers grabbed Helena's head, while Laura took her legs. They moved her to where they had been and chained her to the pole.

A roll of duct tape sat on one of the torturing tables. Laura grabbed and taped her mouth. "We need a hood, in case someone missed the show."

"Are you sure we can't just kill her?"

"Not now."

"Party pooper." Myers pretended to pout. "I don't see any material, but maybe we can just position her so you can't really decipher what you are seeing." He pushed Helena's knees up, placed her head between her knees, and then tied the chain around her.

"There should be two of us." Laura glanced

around. Nothing to make a fake body out of. Wait. "Let's kill the lights, just leave one by this station." One by one, they smashed the lightbulbs. The room fell dark, with the exception of one glowing bulb. "Too much darkness, and they'll come find out why."

They ran to the entrance. Laura had paid attention to the tone of the beeps when they entered. She punched 3-9-7-2. The door clicked open.

The two of them squeezed through and then locked it in place. The boiler room stood before them. They had run around like rats in this maze already. *How does Helena get out of here every day?* "Look for anything on the wall that seems off. There is a code box here somewhere. We just have to find it."

Together, they covered every inch of the enormous room.

"Here," Myers finally said. There was a light panel against a wall.

Laura punched in 3-9-7-2 again, and the door slid to the side. Adrenaline shot through her system. It was a service elevator. They jumped in and hit the next floor. When the door glided open, it revealed a bay of agents. No one seemed to turn her way, so they must be used to having people come and go through here.

Myers whispered, "What now?"

"I have no idea. Blend in?"

The two of them slowly inched forward, eyes darting left and right. If any one person looked up from their activities, Laura would be recognized. A black hat lay on a bunk. She grabbed it and shoved it on her head, then attempted to keep her gaze down as they weaved through the crowd.

"Laura?"

She squeezed her eyes shut, ready to fight, but knowing she did not have the energy to do so well. Slowly, she lifted her head. "Deshawn?"

Myers smiled, grabbed his fist, and pulled him in for a half-hug.

Deshawn pulled back and quickly escorted her and Myers down to a room and pushed them in. It was a broom closet that smelled of bleach and old towels. "Oh my gosh, are you guys back, too?"

"Back *too*?"

"Yeah, they kidnapped me in Mexico and brought me here."

Instinct kicked in. Would he turn them in? Was this a setup? "And you're not locked up?"

Laura and Myers exchanged glances.

"I know, weird, right?"

"Yeah, weird." Laura glanced at Myers again.

"Well, we need to go." Myers started to reach for the handle, but Deshawn blocked the door. "You better get out of my way, man."

"Listen, I know you, Black. You trust no one. But listen. They will kill you if they realize you're here. You are like enemy number one around this place. Your face is on every wall and range target."

"We can't stay in this broom closet. Myers and I have been tortured in this building for I don't even know how long. We need to get out of here, get fed, clean up, and then come back and end this."

Deshawn nodded. "I will help you do that, but let's be smart, okay?"

"Fine. What do you suggest?" Suddenly, Laura felt lightheaded. She started to drop, but Myers caught her.

"You okay?" Deshawn's expression spelled

concern.

"We haven't eaten much in days, little water, and just an IV drip today." Myers held her up against his chest. It felt strong and comforting. A position they had grown accustomed to after every torture session. "And she's pregnant."

"Are you going to tell everybody?"

He laughed. "It saved us last time didn't it?"

"Pregnant? Word," Deshawn said a bit loud.

"Sshh," Laura and Myers said together with fingers to their lips.

Deshawn whispered, "You and Bryce having a baby? That's dope. Does Bryce know?"

Laura's heart sunk. He didn't know. She shook her head.

They remained silent for a moment, then Deshawn said, "Okay...let's take care of basics first. I'll be right back. Lock the door when I leave. I will scratch, not knock." He put his hand on the knob. "Except for a few horny teenagers, only the custodians come in here. Good for you, they are out until tomorrow night." He turned the handle. "Be back. Lock it."

Myers waited until the door closed to get up. He leaned her against a shelf and crossed to lock it. Turning back, he asked, "I know he's my friend, but can we trust him?"

Who knew anymore? Her rate of confidence outside of her regular team was at an all-time low. "I think we have to. Worst case...it is just another of Harding's attempts at letting out the leash. We'll play his game and be back where we were. Or we'll be free."

Myers slid next to her and wrapped his arm around her shoulders. "Best case, we're out of here."

"Yeah, exactly." Laura leaned into him and closed her eyes. "If Harding wanted us dead, we would be six feet under. This is more about breaking us anyway. We'll look for an exit, and we'll take it. If Deshawn is good, we'll take him with us." She opened her eyes and tilted her head up to see Myers. "If he isn't, we'll kill him with the rest."

He stared at her a moment, then nodded.

A strong emotion enveloped her. For a moment, she thought he might kiss her again. Part of her wanted him to. The other part hated that first part. Her husband only died maybe five weeks ago. This man had been like a brother to her. Why was she feeling things for him? She closed her eyes again. Extreme circumstances could do that. Harding had been trying to condition them to join S.I.U., but instead he was conditioning her heart toward Myers. They both endured the worst torture together. Forever, they would be bonded by death and pain.

"Can we address the elephant?"

Laura peered up. "Probably should. Though I'm not sure I want to."

He touched her chin softly. "You know I love you. I always have. Just not like that."

She nodded and tried to look away.

His hand on her chin kept her with him. "But that doesn't mean things don't change."

Her stomach flipped at those words. "I'm scared."

"Yeah, me too." His arms enveloped her. "None of this makes sense, and honestly, I don't think we need to think about it now. Our emotions are all out of whack. You just lost your husband. I lost my girlfriend to Satan. We're sleep-deprived, malnourished, and hurt.

Who knows what we really feel." He kissed the top of her head. "But I know I love you and will protect you and that kid, no matter if that is romantic or platonic. You mean everything to me. Understand?"

"Completely." She turned and hugged him. "And ditto. Well, minus the kid part."

He chuckled.

A scratch sounded on the door.

Myers let her go and stood to open it.

Deshawn ducked in. His arms held two water bottles and a sack. He dropped the sack and distributed the water. "I couldn't get as much as I wanted because the mess hall was closed, but luckily, they had some stuff out in the halls."

Laura practically downed the water bottle, before being handed an apple and a pair of granola bars. Within minutes, she had consumed all there was. "So, you have a plan?"

"Maybe." He collected the wrappers and empty bottles and placed them in the paper sack. "There is a training session this afternoon, we could leave then."

"I think Helena will wake up before that, and they'll know we're gone," Laura said.

Myers shook his head. "Even if she wakes up. We tied her, gagged her, and made the room dark. I think it will buy us some time."

"I hope you're right." Laura met Deshawn's stare. "We're in your hands. Get us home."

Chapter Twenty-Nine

Teddy sat in the hotel room chewing his nails and tapping his foot. This was taking too long. How long was Charlie going to just sit staring at that laptop screen? His hand hadn't even moved in like thirty minutes. Surely, something had to have shown by now. Teddy jumped up, sending the seat almost toppling behind him, and began pacing on the hotel yellow shag rug.

Sitting on the queen-size bed, Eri and Willow giggled like two teen girls at a high school dance. How could they be so happy? It had been more than a month now, and the well had run dry with ideas. This was their fourteenth time stopping to find a hot spot. The longer it took, the more he just knew his missing friends were dead. Shouldn't that raise some kind of urgency? Was he the only one who cared?

"And they always say you're the best," Teddy mumbled.

Charlie peered up from behind the screen with a raised eyebrow. "What's that supposed to mean?"

"Sorry, it's just..." Teddy faced him with hands out at his side. "Come on, man. Lives are at stake. How many more days can we do this? You just staring at your screen as if, *poof*, some magic is going to happen."

Willow must have sensed his unease. She walked

up behind him and laid her frail hand on his waist. "Charlie is doing the best he can. Give him some grace. We're chasing down trained assassins who do not like to be found. Charlie might be good, but there are dozens of Charlies making sure we don't find them."

"I know, I know." Teddy paced away. "It's just, I'm afraid. I mean, let's be real. They're dead, right?"

Charlie leapt up with palms out like two stop signs. "Whoa, dude. No. You have to stop. None of us is going there. We will find them. You just have to chill out and trust me, okay?"

Eri stepped forward and spoke calmly, "If they wanted to kill them, S.I.U. could have ended it in that house. There was something else they wanted. And you know Laura, no amount of torture will work. She'll hold out."

Yes, Laura was good—the best of the best. *Great point.* That gave him a slight glimmer of hope. "I mean, there is also the possibility she could escape, right? She's that awesome. We all know it." He pointed to the laptop. "Have we checked the dating board to see if maybe they escaped?"

"Hourly," Charlie said defeated.

Teddy began to pace again, resuming his meal of fingernails. "She was always kind to me, even when I didn't shut up. She gave me purpose. We have to find her. I don't know what I'd do if something happened. I'm alive because of her. I owe her."

"We all do." Eri touched his arm and smiled. "Maybe we need to take a break and eat. I'm starving."

"I could eat," Teddy agreed.

Charlie shook his head. "You guys go ahead. I'll keep at it."

"Are you feeling ill? You never turn down food." Eri pretended to take his temperature.

"Um, I didn't say I didn't want to eat." He pushed her hand away. "Just bring me something with a lot of grease and sugar."

"Now that is the man I know." Eri kissed the top of his head. "You know, someday that is going to catch up to you."

"That will be the day I eat tofu. Until then, extra cheese and mayo please. And the largest fry."

She kissed her husband again and motioned for Teddy and Willow to follow her out the door. The air outside was thick and hot, the clouds overhead black and billowing. Normally, where Teddy was from, a rainstorm would cool things off. But not here. It just seemed to make the blanket of heat denser and more unbearable. Maybe this all added to his anxiety. They needed to rescue Laura and Myers and move onto cooler digs before it drove him insane.

About one block from the diner, it started to pour. The group laughed as they ducked into the truck stop. A few people lifted their heads at the rowdy entrance, but quickly, returned to their plates of fatty substance. The restaurant smelled of cooking oil and baked bread. It made Teddy's stomach growl.

He pointed to a booth toward the back, away from the windows. They had learned their lesson about sitting in exposed places. He glanced down at his bandaged wrist. The doctor had said he could get his stitches out soon. Not that they would go to another doctor to get them out. Trying to explain to the cops why his hand had a hole in it was not a fun experience.

"Teddy, are you okay?" Willow glanced down at

arm. "Is your wrist bothering you again?"

"I'm fine. I just—" His heart dropped into his stomach at the site in front. A young girl named Kaitlin stood at the counter paying for what looked like a box of donuts. "Oh my gosh." He lifted his menu up and ducked behind.

Willow followed his gaze and then mirrored his action.

"Something I should know?" Eri asked from behind their wall of menus, as she glanced over her shoulder.

"S.I.U. agent."

Eri slid to the wall side of the booth and kicked her legs up, probably to use her peripherals. "The skinny blonde with glasses?"

"Yeah that's her," Teddy said, before peering around the menu and then ducking back again.

"We have to follow her," Eri replied.

"She knows us. We couldn't get within a few feet of her without being made," Willow whispered.

"Then I will follow her."

"What?" Teddy didn't have time to respond.

Eri slid out of the booth and walked to the door just in time to hold it open for Kaitlin. Eri glanced back, winked, and left behind her.

Both lowered their menus and stared at each other in disbelief. Was this a break or just really stupid? "Do you think Kaitlin will head back, or do you think she'll figure out who Eri is?"

Teddy dropped the menu, grabbed Willow's hand, and ran for the entrance. "Either way, we have to get back to Charlie right away. Maybe he can monitor Eri's cell phone. Come on."

The two of them hurried to the door, glanced around, and then bolted back to the hotel down the block. When they reached it, Teddy could hardly breathe. "We have got to work out more."

"Agreed," Willow wheezed.

Teddy slid the card in the slot and entered.

Charlie still sat at the table typing on his laptop. Eyes still focused on the screen, he said, "That was fast. Did you bring me enough greas—" He looked up and stood, fear apparent in his expression. "Where's Eri? Why are you wheezing? What happened? Where's my wife?"

"Kaitlin. A girl we know from—" Teddy grabbed his thighs, trying to catch his breath.

"Yes, a girl we knew from—" Willow breathed.

"S.I.U., she—"

"S.I.U.?" Charlie's eyes grew wide with panic. "Eri, where is Eri?"

Teddy grabbed both of Charlie's shoulders and smiled. "Eri is following an operative. We know her. Can you ping her cell?"

He didn't hesitate. Charlie straddled his chair and alternated between typing and clicking the mouse. Within seconds, he had her.

"What should we do?" Teddy asked.

Charlie reached in his duffle bag and handled out earpieces. "Here, put these in and start walking. I'll guide you to her."

"Got it." Teddy tucked a gun in his belt and handed another one to Willow. "Let's go get our friends back."

Chapter Thirty

Helena opened her eyes. Her head throbbed, and the space was dark. All her muscles complained. *Why?* She tried to discern her situation; ironically, it was something Laura had once taught her to do. Chains rattled in the dark when she moved her wrists. Her body was bent over, unable to straighten. Her mouth was held shut, probably taped. Panic enveloped her. She tried to move but couldn't.

What could she do? The room was too dark to discern much. They must have busted out the lights. *Stupid Harding and Alicia. If they weren't so busy playing "patty cake" in the control room, maybe they would have seen the betrayal.* Unless that is what Harding wanted—to kill Helena and have his precious Laura back in the fold. Hatred seethed through Helena's entire being. She loathed this place. Despised everyone in it. Maybe more than Laura. *They can all go to—*

The door squeaked opened. Helena tried to yell through the tape.

"Why is it so dark in here?" It was Alicia. "Hello? What are you dumb kids up to now?"

Helena thrashed about, moaning. "Abisha…"

Alicia sauntered over to her, heels clicking on the cement floor, and shined a flashlight on Helena's face. Her eyes widened. "What the…?" She hurried to the desk in the far left corner and found the key to the chain. It took a few tries, but finally, the lock clicked open.

Helena fell over, her muscles locked and in pain, unable to fully work yet. She reached for the tape on her mouth and pulled. She grimaced at the sting.

"What happened?" Alicia demanded.

"Our friends happened while you were busy sucking face." Helena lifted, but couldn't stand. "Come on. Help me up. We have some vermin to exterminate."

Alicia reached for her arm and helped her to stand.

Helena's legs wobbled in complaint. "Come on, body, and cooperate. We have to hurry."

"They won't get beyond the boiler room, so I'm sure it will be fine." Alicia waved at the air.

With narrowed eyes, Helena faced her partner, blood searing with an incredible amount of rage. "Have you lived with the same Laura I have? You know she is resourceful. While you and Harding were doing God knows what in the control room, she managed to best me and get out of this room. Most likely, she is half way to Mexico right now."

"Fine. Okay." Alicia wrapped Helena's arm around her neck for support. "No reason to get testy. We'll get her. And you really should be happy."

"What?" Helena shook her head, not sure if she could handle being with this woman one more second. "Why on earth would I be happy?"

"Because if she is really escaping, you'll get your wish." A big smile flashed on Alicia's face. "You can shoot her."

A few steps out the door and Helena already felt better. The girl was right. That did make her happy.

Helena unwrapped from Alicia's hold and tested her legs. *Good enough.* "I'm fine. Let's go."

They rushed the back way to the control tower, as fast as Helena could manage. The hallway never seemed so long. Had it always been this dark and squeaky? Finally, they were standing outside the immense metal door. Alicia punched in the code on the wall keypad and waited for it to slide to the side, before entering.

Helena followed her in.

Harding sat at his desk typing on a computer keyboard and watching the letters appear on the monitor. "How are our prisoners doing?" he asked without looking up.

"Gone," Helena said with contained emotion.

"What?" Harding's gaze slowly met hers, menacing, scary. "What do you mean gone?"

"They tied me up in their place and escaped. That's what I mean *gone*." Helena crossed her arms and stared him down, then added with a bit of sass, "And thanks for noticing on your monitors, by the way. Good thing we had all those cameras in there, or we might have missed the whole thing."

He shifted his gaze. The screens were blackened, with the exception of a small light in the back corner. For a moment, he just stared at them, as if something would happen. Then he tapped them three times and faced Alicia. "Sound the alarm."

Both girls stood still.

"Now," he demanded.

Helena went to the monitors and hit the red switch on the right of them. An ear-piercing screech sounded down the hall and throughout the building. Lights flashed from the corners. The S.I.U. agents would all run for the armory. They had practiced this drill a million times since Washington D.C.—the last time S.I.U. fell due to Black's hands. This place would be like Fort Knox in a matter of seconds. No one in. No one out. Shoot to kill anyone who was with Laura Black.

Harding cocked the gun in his hand and motioned to the door. "I want her alive, Helena. Do you hear me?"

"Yeah, sure. I get it. But if she fires on me, I have to fire back."

"Then you better hope she doesn't miss. Because if you kill her, you will join her." He pushed Helena out the door and then passed her in a run. The three of them sprinted through the boiler room to the secret door. Inside, all students now stood at attention in rows with guns. When Harding entered, all turned in unison sounding a deafening cadence of boots hitting the floor.

"At ease and listen up."

In unison, the group shifted their arms and legs to parade rest.

"Our enemy has somehow once again penetrated our facility. She is not to be killed but brought to me alive. Do you understand?"

A loud "yes sir" echoed through the space.

"However, you may kill anyone with her."

"No," Helena said, before she could hold it in.

Harding glowered at her before marching to her side. He jammed a gun hard under her chin, causing her head to push back. "If you defy me again, Agent, I will pull the trigger. Understood?"

Tears seeped from her eyes, both from pain and

fear. She nodded, knowing he meant it.

He shoved her hard against the wall and walked past her. The impact shot pain up her spine. She closed her eyes for a moment to get her bearings.

"Now, start looking everywhere." Harding waved his gun at the group of soldiers. "Every nook, every cranny. She's here somewhere. Find her, and I'll make it worth your while. Now go!"

The squad fanned out as they moved throughout the corridor. Teenagers with rifles lined every hallway. Many of them paraded through rooms and closets, looking for the enemy. Helena followed close behind, watching, in some ways hoping they didn't find her.

A part of Helena wanted to find Myers and Laura first. She could shoot Laura and save Myers. But both of those choices would get her killed. Maybe she could help Myers and Laura escape and kill Laura later. Yes, that was the perfect plan. Would they even trust her to let that happen? And longer term, would Myers ever forgive her? Could he ever be hers again? Or would it be for nothing?

Hot tears streamed down her face. At once, she hated all of it. That included herself. There was nothing good left in her. All of that was stolen so long ago. Could she blame Myers for hating her? She hated herself.

She ducked under bunks and looked in stairwells, closets, and offices. Every man was on deck doing the same. Where were they? Helena needed to find them first. That was one thing she knew. What happened after, Helena would figure out then.

Chapter Thirty-One

Laura heard the alarms go off just as Myers and Deshawn neared an exit. Both their eyes went wide. Deshawn ran his badge frantically against the door. Little red lights flickered, then nothing. Again. Nothing.

"Lock down. We're not going anywhere." Deshawn stepped back and ran a hand over his head. "Protocol states that if an intruder, such as Black, gets in, no one in and no one out. Kill anyone caught with Black but bring her back alive."

Myers raised an eyebrow. "You're saying they planned for this?"

"Every day, it seems. The few people I talked to said they knew Laura would be back, and it became part of the training exercises."

Laura shook her head. "We didn't come here. They brought us here." This all didn't make sense. Or did it. Did Harding know she'd escape? He had to have. No one would know more than him. But what was his plan? "We need to hide. Suggestions?"

Deshawn didn't answer, just began walking back down the hall. They followed him to a grate, where he motioned for them to follow him in. Myers was the last one in and closed them up. They crawled down a shaft to an opening. Deshawn pushed a lever and the floor of the shaft opened revealing a ladder down a long tube.

He smiled and jumped in. Laura once again prayed this wasn't some elaborate trap. But what choice did they have? She swung her leg over the side and lowered herself down. Myers followed right behind her.

The tube ended outside a hatch door. Deshawn pushed down on the wheel. It wouldn't budge. He glanced at Myers. Myers nodded and together the two of them got the rusted metal wheel to open. They stepped inside what looked like an old bomb shelter decorated in the 1970s. It housed an old-style TV, a couch, and a record player. The walls were made out of brown paneling, and the floor was covered in an awful rust shag carpet. At the end of the bunker were shelves packed with food and water.

"What is this place?" Laura picked up a yellow wrapped can marked "Soda" in black letters. All the cans were matching with different titles.

"I'm not sure, but I made out with a hot high-ranking agent down here once." Deshawn winked at Myers knowingly.

Myers laughed.

"And you didn't think to ask her what this was?"

Myers and Deshawn exchanged glances and chuckled.

"Men and their hormones. Whatever." Laura paced in the small area. "What I'm worried about is if they will think to look for us here?"

Myers stepped over to the wall and played with the controls. "No way."

"What?" Laura came up behind him and placed a hand on his shoulder.

"Do you know what this is?"

"Enlighten me."

He spun around to face her, only inches away. Their eyes locked and Laura swallowed. "What is it?" her voice cracked a bit.

"It's a safe room," Myers said.

"And that's good because…?"

A big grin encompassed his face. "Because it means I can change the code, and we can stay here for quite some time." He punched a few keys and several monitors lowered from the ceiling. Cameras caught all areas of the compound, including outside their door.

"This is amazing!" Excited, Laura kissed Myers hard on the cheek.

His smile faded, serious, but not mad. He stared at her a moment, looking like he might say something, but instead, walked past her. "I'm going to see if there is a bathroom behind those cases." He walked around them and disappeared.

Deshawn walked to Laura's side. "Can I ask you something without getting punched?"

Laura laughed. "Yeah, why would I punch you?"

"I see the way you look at him."

"Who?"

Deshawn nodded to the where Myers had gone.

"Myers? Don't be ridiculous."

Deshawn peered over at the cases. "Yeah, well, you can deny it, but I see what I see. I thought you and Bryce were married. I mean, I know you've been locked up together and all, but…"

Laura's joy sunk into her chest. The mention of Bryce's name stung. "Bryce is dead." Those words dropped heavy in the room. Shock was evident on Deshawn's face. It quickly turned to sadness. He bent down to the ground, hovering on his haunches. "How?"

Emotion grasped Laura's throat as she tried to respond. "Helena murdered him."

"Man! That's... I can't even... There are no words." Deshawn closed his eyes and exhaled through his nose. "I wondered what happened when I saw her. She didn't say hi and was saying things about being loyal to S.I.U. I thought she was tripping, like they had her on something." Deshawn stood and put out his arms for a hug. "I'm so sorry, Laura. We all loved that guy."

Laura hugged him and nodded. "Thank you."

The sound of running water sounded in the other room.

"I hope they can't hear that," Laura said in some hopes of changing the subject.

"I don't think so. It's pretty solid steel in here." Deshawn slapped the wall. "My guess it was built to withstand blowing this place up."

That sounded like Harding. Get all the agents rushing around, and he hides in here while they are annihilated. Laura walked to the shelf and grabbed a yellow can marked "water" and popped it open. The water was sweet and cool. It didn't take but a minute to down the entire thing.

Myers walked back in, drying his head, wearing an olive drab T-shirt and black shorts.

"So, you found a shower." Laura grinned.

Myers shot a towel at her thigh.

It snapped but didn't hurt. "Hmm, you'll pay for that."

"Just go shower. You stink."

Laura narrowed her eyes, playfully. "Fine. Only because you're right." She ducked around the corner. A small stand-up shower only big enough for one thin body stood on the left, only inches away from a super short toilet. It reminded her of the toilets in elementary school. There was no sink. So, all the water must come from the shower. She flipped on the handle and water poured down. It was lukewarm. After a minute, it seemed it would not get any warmer, so she underdressed and stepped inside.

The water streamed down her body, stinging against the open scratches and sores. But it soothed her. She closed her eyes and breathed in. Symbolically, it was like washing away all the bad from the past few days. They needed their strength if they were to fight their way out. Right now, they would be taken—most likely killed. For some reason, Laura was supposed to live. And that was before Harding knew of her pregnancy. So, that wasn't enough. Myers and Deshawn could not die; that was not an option. She would not lose another friend in this fight.

She glanced down at her naked abdomen. It had started to swell. Lately, she had felt twinges in her stomach, like bubbles. Through all the trauma of the last month, she hoped the baby was okay. It appeared he or she still grew.

She shut off the water and stepped out. A towel lay on the toilet seat, along with some clothes. Funny, she didn't remember that there before. Myers must have put it there. She smiled as she pulled on the olive drab T-shirt and gray sweat pants. Luckily, they had a string, as they were a bit big. She probably looked like a girl playing dress up in her father's clothes. She started to walk around the corner, when she overheard her name.

"So, you and Laura, huh?" Deshawn asked.

"No, man, it isn't like that."

"Yeah, right. You just keep telling yourself that. I see the way you two look at each other."

Myers sighed. "I can't hurt her, man. She means too much for me to make that mistake."

"What do you mean?"

"I mean, her heart belongs to Bryce. I could never replace that. I wouldn't want to try."

Deshawn chuckled. "Man, you have it bad."

"Did you just hear what I said?"

"Oh, I hear you. But body language says way more. I get it. You don't want to move in on Bryce's wife, but he's gone. You've lost someone, and she's lost someone. It's really okay. No one in this family would fault either of you for liking each other." The sound of a slap happened, likely on Myer's back. "Follow your heart. You two are going to need each other, especially with that kid on the way."

Laura closed her eyes. What did she think? In a way, she felt numb. Her stomach twisted and turned. Could she be falling for Myers? It was true; they had been through a lot together. It was possible that was all this was—a bond formed due to vile conditions. Of course, they would always love each other. But could they *love* each other. She didn't know. Nor did she want to figure that out just now. Laura took a deep breath, stepped back a few steps, and started forward with hard steps that would be heard. "That shower was amazing."

Myers peered at her over the top of a couch pillow and grinned. "I can't smell you from here, so I would say it did its job. Nice clothes by the way."

"Thanks." She punched him in the arm and dropped next to him. "So, what now?"

Chapter Thirty-Two

Laura opened her eyes and realized she must have fallen asleep in Myers' lap. His hand combed through her hair as he stared off in space. Slowly, she rose and began tilting her neck side to side to remove the kink. "How long was I out?"

"About an hour." Myers yawned. "I tried but couldn't get comfortable."

"Apparently, you were the only one." Laura pointed to Deshawn who snored on a cot in the corner. "I think he's louder than you."

Myers tickled her.

She grabbed his hand to stop him, laughing.

Their hands intertwined. Her heart raced. Shivers shot through her system. There was more here than she would admit. It was apparent, and she knew he felt it, too. His stare grew serious. His lips parted and met hers. She didn't push away. They were warm, inviting. Tears welled in her eyes. So much emotion overwhelmed her. He pulled back and touched her cheek with his thumb. "I'm sorry. I don't want to hurt you."

She shook her head. "You didn't. I'm just confused."

"Yeah, and that's why I'm sorry." He tucked a strand of hair behind her ear. "You mean the world to me. I don't want to make things worse."

"I know there is something happening between us. I'm not going to deny it." She pulled a couch pillow into her lap and began toying with its tag. "I'm just not ready to face it head on. Get me out of here. Let me grieve properly, and then we'll see."

He wrapped his arm around her and pulled her into him. "Deal."

Now how to break the tension? "Is there reception in this place?" She nodded to the TV.

"No, but there is an assortment of movies saved." He reached for the remote and hit *on*. A menu popped on the screen. "So, action, sci-fi, or romance?"

They both said, "Sci-fi" together, and laughed.

Halfway through the horror of flesh-eating aliens, Myers touched her hand and faced her. "Bryce was like a brother to me, and you were his wife."

"I know." Laura clicked the remote to pause the movie and faced him. "It's okay if you and me...if we...well, don't—"

He held up a hand and half-smiled. "No, what I mean is. You're stuck with me. I will forever have your back. You're my responsibility now, no matter what."

Though sweet, that humored her. "How chivalrous, but you do know I can take care of myself."

His mouth stayed serious. "You know what I mean."

"Is that the reason you are drawn to me? Out of obligation?" she whispered.

He reached for her hand and laced his fingers with hers. "If only it were that simple."

An overwhelming chemistry pooled between them again. Other than with Bryce, she had never felt this way about a guy before. This was different. And she was glad. She didn't want to compare Myers to Bryce. They were different. The relationship should be too. But nothing would happen if they stayed here. A newfound adrenaline pumped through her body. It could be the five sports coolers she drank to restore electrolytes, or it could be the man next to her, but she was ready.

"Us against the world, Myers." She brushed her lips against his cheek and then looked him square in the eye. "I'm tired of running, of hiding, of mourning. That is my whole life, and I am ready to make a change."

A huge smile slipped across his face. "What do you have in mind?"

"There is no way Harding would have this bunker without a docking station, right? Find the computer, and we clue in our allies." Laura walked to Deshawn's side and shook him.

Yawning, he rolled over, rubbing his eyes. "Yeah. What's up?"

"Help us find the computer."

"Yeah, okay." Deshawn pointed to an upholstered storage bench. "I saw one in there."

Myers walked to it and opened it. Sure enough, a laptop lay inside. Myers lifted it out and grinned. Charlie was often used as the computer geek in their family, but Myers could hold his own around technology. Laura knew about his cyber crimes; after all, she plucked him from jail all those years ago.

Myers rubbed his hands together before hitting a few keys. "I'm in. What should I type?"

"Let Charlie know exactly where we are. Also, he should know we are able to withstand anything where we are at." Laura paced a few steps and then turned back. "And find a channel we can chat on securely."

Myers typed in their coded message on the fake dating site and pushed send. His eyes met hers. "Now we wait."

Chapter Thirty-Three

Teddy stared at the metal gate. It appeared the exterior was completely surrounded by an electric fence. Already, Charlie had disabled two cameras. "So, please tell me we can get in there."

"With a little luck," Charlie sighed, taping ferociously on his laptop on top of the car's hood.

"We really need a new car," Eri said, pacing next to it. The entire side was riddled with bullet holes.

"Rescue my partner in crime, Myers, and I'll get you whatever you want." Charlie winked.

"Get me inside, and I'll get you whatever *you* want." Eri smiled back.

The gate rolled back, revealing two guards. Teddy shot both before they could react. "Well, not the most stealth entrance, but we're in. Shall we?" Teddy held out his looped arm for Eri. She laughed and grabbed it. "Keep us safe, Charlie."

"Get me eyes inside, and I will."

The two of them ran for the entrance, ducking for cover behind a clump of trees. The building in front of them was an enormous mansion surrounded by trees and bushes. Smaller houses sat on the left and right of it. Most likely, they would be housed in the main center.

"Do you hear that?" Eri stopped and cupped her

ear.

Teddy did the same. "A siren inside."

"They've escaped. Come on." Eri ran from cover to cover, rolling, jumping, leaping, and running from tree to bush until she was against the wall. Without warning, she disappeared on the roof and out of sight. If only Teddy could be as smooth. He could climb, but not like her. He touched his earpiece. "So, I take it we're not going in the front door."

Eri laughed. "Hardly. Try and keep up."

Teddy ran at the wall, kicked off, and leapt up to a small ledge just above. Using that, he swung his body to a small side roof. He jogged forward and stopped. An agent cocked his gun. Teddy raised his hands, just as Eri round-kicked the man in the back of the head. He slid down to the ground into a mound of bushes.

"Nice."

"I try." She ran forward and onto the next level.

Teddy followed.

"I'm in," came Charlie's voice through the earpiece. "I've taken control of the camera in the room next to where you are. Do you see the window?"

"Yes." Eri tried to open it, but it wouldn't budge. She pulled out a device to open it, when gunfire whizzed by Teddy's head, just missing Eri.

Teddy flipped around and fired. The man dropped. "We have to hurry."

"I can't get it."

Teddy peeked in the window. It looked like an office. Red strobe lights flickered in the distance. "They are on lock down. We'll never get in."

"And do we want to? Obviously, they are trying to get out." Eri touched her earpiece. "What do you think,

Charlie? Do we keep trying to get in, or just wait for them to come out?"

"Come back for now. I think we need more recon."

"Sounds good." Eri shoved her tools back in her black cargo pants and nodded. "Let's go."

****

Teddy was discouraged, but he was trying not to be a nuisance. Though he was a chatterbox, he was also quite self-aware. Often, he felt the frustration when his nerves got the better of him. How much longer would they have to wait to rescue their friends? Charlie's way was not working. *Enough!* He had to go back. Without asking, Teddy began packing gear on his body.

"What are you doing?" Eri asked, looking over her shoulder from the passenger seat of their vehicle.

"We can't just sit here all day. The longer we wait, the more likely it is they are dead." He pulled a bulletproof vest over his head and fastened the two Velcro sides.

"Look, I know you're anxious. We all are, but—"

"I have them," Charlie said from the front.

Teddy stopped and leaned forward. "What? Where?"

"The dating site." Charlie shifted around to see each of them. "They are holed up in some kind of bunker, completely safe, but trapped."

"So, we need to create a distraction?" Teddy smiled.

Willow returned the grin. "Anything else?"

"One sec." Charlie tapped a few keys and hit return. "Yes!"

"What?" everyone said in unison.

"We are connected via chat."

"Is it secure?" Eri asked.

Charlie rolled his eyes. "Please, woman. After all these years—"

She punched his arm. "Fine. Do your thing…with a little less sass."

He laughed. "I'll try." Charlie turned on the text speech, so everyone could hear. Then he said as he typed, "Hey, Myers and Laura. Are you okay?"

"Yes, we are good," the computer translated. "We are trapped, but safe."

"We're glad to hear that. Here with Willow, Teddy, and Eri."

The computer said, "Here with Deshawn."

Everyone exchanged glances. Charlie typed, "Deshawn?"

"Yes, he was kidnapped and brought here. Has been helping us. Need to break him out with us."

"Do you trust him?" Charlie said as he typed.

"You know we trust only you, but at this point, we are placing blind faith. We think he's cool."

Charlie nodded, as if Myers could see him.

"Ask him, what now?" Teddy asked.

Charlie typed.

"Distraction," the computer answered.

"What we thought. Do you know what end of the building you are at?"

"Guessing northwest corner."

The group turned to each other, each obviously contemplating a plan. Several lame ideas were tossed out but were easily shaken off. Teddy started to open his mouth, when the computer spoke again.

"Explosion possible. Bunker will withstand."

"What? No!" Teddy shook his head. "There are

good people in there. That doesn't sound like Myers. Are we sure that's Myers? I'm not. Ask him something only he or Laura would know."

Charlie nodded and turned to the keyboard. "Last year, where did we stay the night with just you, me, and Eri?"

There was a long pause, then the computer said, "The Petrova Estate."

Teddy breathed loudly through his nose. "That was a long pause. Why was that a long pause? Did he or she have to go torture someone to get that answer?"

"Why the long pause?" Charlie shrugged, obviously giving into Teddy's anxiety attack.

"Laura was on keyboard."

"Sorry, need to establish it's you. One for Laura. What was the first thing Laura did when she met Charlie?"

"Shoot his keyboard."

"Is that true?" Eri asked.

"Yes." Charlie laughed. "We will figure out a plan and get back to you shortly." He snapped the laptop closed and faced the group. "Okay, any ideas that do not include blowing up this mansion?"

An eerie smile played across Willow's face. "What if we make the fire and police departments come here?"

"What is the protocol for S.I.U. if we do that?" Charlie looked at Willow, since she was obviously the highest ranking and the longest in service for the agency.

"They are obviously on lockdown, so they would know it was a ruse. I don't know, to tell you the truth. But it is worth a shot, right?" Willow reached for Teddy's hand. "How should we do it?"

Eri slid her finger across the screen of her cell phone and dialed 9-1-1. It rang through the speaker, so each one of them could hear.

"9-1-1 operator. What is your emergency?"

"Hurry." *Cough, cough.* "The entire building is going to explode." *Cough, cough.* "They've trapped us inside. Hundreds of teenagers will die. Lots of fire."

"Where are you calling from?"

Eri rattled off the address and then said, "Please, hurry, there are hundreds trapped and some really bad…" She ended the call and then looked at them and smiled. "It's more dramatic that way."

"Let's get ready. When they arrive, we need to be inside. I'll stay here at the computer and vehicle, the rest of you—" Charlie looked to every eye. "Bring them back."

Chapter Thirty-Four

Helena's cell phone buzzed in her pocket. She pulled it out and read the display. It was Harding. *Meet in my office.* That could go either way. Maybe he found them, or maybe he would punish her. There was never any indication of what his plan was. After he had placed that gun under her chin, she was now frightened of him.

The office was about a minute from her position. She pushed past the various soldiers and made her way down the corridor. The outside door was ajar. She peeked in. Harding sat at his desk. She rapped on the door. "Hi. It's me, Helena."

"Wait until I call you," he said without looking up. The reverberating sound of disappointment sounded in his voice. This would not go well.

She closed the door and began to pace. Why had he sent for her? The entire place was abuzz with trying to find their enemy. Most of them believed Laura and Myers must have gotten out. After all, three agents were dead outside and no one new had entered the building. Helena was starting to agree.

"Helena, get in here," Harding yelled through the cracked door.

She rushed in and stood at attention at the end of his desk. "Yes, sir."

"Good. It's about time you remembered how to talk to me." He nodded to the door. "Close it and sit down."

She complied. This whole thing made her nervous. People died for less. Laura and Myers were her responsibility, and they had escaped. Chances are, he'd kill her for it. It had been quite apparent all day that any favor was long spent.

"Some people think Black and Luther got out of here, but I know my old partner. She's still here. Lurking, seeking her revenge. I can sense her." Harding scratched his goatee and leaned forward. "I also know her friends are in a green car a few blocks down the street from here. They are the reason some of my men are dead outside."

That made her heart rate increase. Helena did not want to face Teddy or Willow. Really, any of them. They had to hate her. Eri would kill her without blinking. An overwhelming sense of guilt was lingering, and that would just make it worse. But she was a professional. She better get on board, before he remembered she was responsible for Laura's exodus. "So, what do you want me to do, sir?"

"I'm going to the bunker along with the best of our men." He stood and tucked a batch of papers in a briefcase, before looking at her. "And you, my friend, are going to blow this place up for me."

"Blow this place up?" Her stomach soured. "But, sir, there are close to three hundred people in this facility."

"All replaceable."

She stared at him, stunned. Evil oozed from him. Why had she followed this vile man down into hell?

"Do you have a problem with this? Or shall I kill you and do it myself?" If Helena ever wondered what the devil looked like, she knew now. She could see it in his dark, narrowed eyes. How could he kill all these people? He walked around the front of the desk and faced her. "I need an answer."

"Will it kill Laura?"

A sardonic smile crossed his face. "Likely."

"I thought you didn't want to kill her?"

He crossed his arms and leaned back against the desk. "Honestly, I knew you wanted to kill her, and that was enough for me not to allow it. You need to learn proper respect. You have made so many slipups, Helena. And in simple terms, S.I.U. does not allow any mistakes. You know this." He shook his head and pasted on a derisive grin she had learned to loath. "Always following your hatred of Laura, which is so dumb, since Laura didn't even pull the trigger."

Helena's jumped to her feet. "What?"

Harding got up from the desk and circled her. His mouth came within an inch of her ear, and he whispered, "*I* fired the kill shot." He walked a few feet away and turned back to face her. "She only wounded him. When she saw you coming, she was going to stop. So, I brought the mission to fruition. We had orders— kill."

Stars flashed in Helen's vision. Her head swam. Everything she had done for the last few years crashed around her. Without warning, her legs gave out, and she buckled to the floor. "You killed my father?"

"Yes, yes, I did. Not by my order, of course. It was still Greenstone's call, but I pulled the trigger." He grabbed her chin and forced her head up to look at him.

"And the beauty of that action was it helped me control you."

As that soaked into her brain, her body heated with fury. She reached for her gun, but Harding was ready. He slapped it across the room, then brought his own weapon hard against her shoulder and fired. Pain shot through her entire left side. Air sucked from her lungs. Blood pooled around her knees.

"So here it is, my dutiful dog." Harding walked in front of her and knelt down, gun hanging in front of him. "You will blow up this place, because I said so. This is not a negotiation. It never was. You have never had power here. I have always held the chain, and you have been a not-so-good dog. I used to own a dog. And when they don't comply, when they bite the hand that feeds them, do you know what happens?"

Helena didn't answer. Couldn't answer. Hot tears streamed down her cheeks. Any moment, she may vomit. None of this made sense.

"I'll tell you what happens. We put them to sleep." He shoved the gun to her head and pulled the trigger. It snapped. Empty. Her stomach knotted, and she leaned forward and vomited on the carpet.

"Gross. I'd say clean it, but then it won't matter. I suppose you thought that was it. The kill shot?" He laughed. "I only put one bullet in the chamber. I love a good game of Russian roulette, don't you? No, the bullet is in your shoulder. Only one, because I can't go killing my dog before it completes the biggest trick yet."

"I'm not doing anything for you," she cried. "Kill me. I don't care."

"Oh, I intend to." Harding walked to his desk and

pulled out the bottom desk drawer. For a second, he rummaged around before removing a device attached to a lever. He joined her again, pushed it in her good hand, and forced her fingers over it. "Now, don't let go too soon, my dear. Wouldn't want to blow both of us up, now do we?"

"I will kill you," Helena said through gritted teeth.

"Not if I kill you first." Harding grabbed a detonator from the desk and clicked on a timer that started with the number twenty. "This entire office is set to explode. If you drop that once I'm gone, it will go early. Good luck."

Within seconds, he was gone. Helena couldn't move. Her body burned, weak from the bullet that had gone through her side. Her good hand held tight. Reality flooded her. She killed that nice man, Julio. Shot Denise. Murdered Bryce. Betrayed Laura and Myers, for what? A lie. All this time, she served the man who had actually killed her father. Her body wracked with sobs. Tears blinded her. How could she have been so stupid? Part of her wanted to let go of the lever. End it all. It was pointless now. She could never have Myers or Laura's forgiveness. She had stolen everything from them.

An explosion sounded from outside. Helena flinched. She scooted on the floor to the window and used her head to slide back the curtain. A fire burned in one of the trees on the east side of the complex. The Calvary was likely here to make a distraction. Little did they know, in nineteen or so minutes, this entire place would blow with them in it. Could she warn them somehow? Maybe do one right thing before she died?

Helena crawled to desk. She tried to get up on the

chair, but it rolled beneath her. Three times, she slipped and fell, pain shooting through her system each try. One last time, with a big breath, pinning the chair against the wall, she struggled again. This time it worked. She was in.

Unable to use her dead weight arm, she used her nose to push the mouse. Then an idea occurred to her. There was a pencil holder on the desk that was the same circumference of the lever to the detonator. Could she put the detonator inside the cup without discharging the clip? She had to try. Using her face, her hand, and even the floppy appendage, she managed to pull it over and insert it. She squeezed her eyes shut and let go. It didn't open. *Yes!*

Now to warn Charlie. She typed into the dating site and wrote, "Dear Charles, I know I wasn't the date you expected, and I do not expect you to understand. I know I cannot be forgiven. For this reason, do not come to see me. For it will be quite an explosion, and none of us are ready for that. Better to wait for another day. Sincerely, Aneleh."

Now to get out of here. Warm and tacky blood seeped down her body. She had little energy left. Her extremities were growing cold. Could she make it?

The door opened. It was Alicia.

"Helena? Oh my gosh!"

"He shot me. He shot my father." Helena gurgled before passing out.

Chapter Thirty-Five

Teddy blinked to clear his vision. Though hardly ever allowed, he was manning the laptop for a few hours, while Charlie took a nap. Teddy didn't mind because it helped to keep his mind off what was really happening; he was hopeful something would change and become better. What he really wanted to do was go in and rescue his friends, but Charlie would not allow it. He said it was more likely they would lose him, than get back the other three. In most scenarios, that was probably true.

In the corner, an alert for the dating service pinged. Teddy sat up and smiled. "Charlie, wake up." He clicked on the digital envelope, and it expanded the screen. His eyes scanned the note. "We have a message, but it's not Laura."

Everyone in the vehicle sat forward, expectant.

Charlie slid forward, grabbed the laptop from Teddy's knee, and opened the document. "Oh my gosh."

"What?" they all asked in unison.

"It's from Helena."

"Then ignore it." Eri sat back and closed her eyes.

Charlie shook his head. "I don't think we can. She's telling us to stay away and says they are going to blow this place up."

Teddy peered out the window as blue and red lights flashed down the distant street. The sound of sirens followed the lights. "At least the firemen and cops got our message from the burning trees. I would say they are about two minutes out. Maybe they can help with this situation. Should we email Laura back? Make sure she knows?"

"Maybe," Charlie said, clicking around on his computer.

"Is that his end game? To blow all of this up?" Willow asked frantically. "This can't be it, right? Did we trigger something? Is this on us? Our fault?"

Teddy laced his fingers with hers and squeezed. "This is not solely our fault. We may have triggered it, but only a sick individual would think to carry it out."

Eri nodded. "No truer words. This is not on us."

"But why blow it up? This is S.I.U."

"Most likely he has another headquarters." Teddy leaned his head out the window to get a better look at the property. "We know there were at least three."

"But all those innocent people." Willow's eyes pooled with tears. "Most of them haven't even finished puberty yet. We have to do something. Just like you rescued us in Washington D.C. We have to do the same here."

Charlie glanced her and held her gaze for a moment before nodding. "Okay, give me a second." He began clicking keys. At once, a blood-curdling alarm sounded in the building, and the doors opened. Water could be seen pouring from the ceilings inside. Young agents began darting across the grass away from the building.

The fire truck, along with an ambulance and a

215

police car, drove to the front gate. Charlie hacked that too, and the gate swung wide, allowing them entry. The emergency service personnel pulled in and parked in a circle in front of the building. It was total chaos, as the response team obviously tried to determine what was happening.

"Now what?" Eri said.

"Nothing yet. Right now, I guess we wait to see." Charlie popped open an energy drink and took a sip.

"Wait? But our friends…" Willow stared out the window. "Please, guys, we have to do something."

Teddy silently prayed their guys got out in time. One silver lining, Laura had said they could survive an explosion where they were at, but even still. "I'm in agreement with Willow. I don't think we should *wait and see what happens*." Teddy mocked Charlie's tone. "We should go in."

"Look, from what we know they are in a safe place and Helena warned us—" Charlie started.

"Helena? Bryce's murderer." Teddy raised an eyebrow. "Seriously? That is what you are using as quality intel here? The ultimate betrayer who has one desire—to kill our good friend Laura Black? Pahlease." Teddy opened his door and stepped out on the sidewalk. Out of nowhere, an agent kicked him in the chest. His body flew against a neighborhood car, knocking the wind out of him.

Eri, Charlie, and Willow leapt out of the other open doors and ran toward the assailant. Eri slid over the hood of car and bashed into him. The guy slammed to the pavement, just as two more took his place.

The next guy swung at Teddy. He ducked and swung back. His fist made contact. Blood trickled from the attacker's brow as the guy raised a gun.

Willow palmed a knife and tossed it at the guy. It landed in his neck, dropping him to the pavement.

Charlie also spared with one, both blocking, until the guy flipped behind him and raised a gun to his head.

Eri darted over the top of the car and dove toward him. His body plummeted hard to the sidewalk. She stood over him and jammed her boot in the man's throat. "Nobody points a gun at my guy."

The man's eyes fluttered, and then he fell unconscious.

Charlie laughed. "You know that was super cheesy, right?"

She winked. "Yeah, but so fun."

"I really am married to the baddest girl." They came together and began kissing.

Willow saddled up next to Teddy.

"Took them long enough to find us." Teddy wrapped an arm around Willow. "I would have thought they would have been out here hours ago."

Charlie looked away from his wife and smiled. "Yeah, it did take them a while."

"What should we do with them?" Willow asked.

"Leave them. Look!" Teddy pointed to the front of the building, shocked at who he saw coming their way.

Alicia appeared to be struggling to carry Helena in her arms. Her "sister" did not look well. Her body was covered in blood. Her eyes closed and face ashen.

"Should we drop them?" Eri readied her gun.

A pair of paramedics crossed their line of fire, heading for the two women with a rolling gurney.

Eri lowered her gun. "Great."

"Helena didn't look good. Maybe she's already

done for." Teddy touched her back. "We can hope. Right?"

"Laura will not like the fact they made it out." Eri shoved her gun in her waistband and reclined against the hood of the car.

The paramedic motioned for a gurney to be moved toward an ambulance. The man and his partner hoisted the rolling bed onto the back of their vehicle and began administering first aid.

Alicia stood guard, glancing around. Her eyes fell to the group. Their gazes locked, both knowing this battle was not over. In some ways, Teddy sensed her fear. Their Camelot had fallen. Soon their prince would too. She stepped up next to the EMT, who then closed the door. With sirens blazing, within minutes, the vehicle was gone.

"Charlie, you have to monitor where they are going. If Laura makes it out alive—" Eri started.

"You mean, when?" Teddy crossed his arms. "You mean, when she makes it out alive. Right?"

Eri nodded. "Of course. *When* Laura makes it out alive, she is going to want to know where they are. We have to do whatever it takes to end this. If not, she'll always been haunting us."

"I think Alicia is the bigger threat," Willow said.

Charlie nodded. "I agree. I mean, I could be wrong, but I think she was the mastermind behind most of it."

"Are they even sisters?" Teddy wondered out loud.

"Probably not," Charlie responded.

"So, are we going in now, or what?" Teddy asked.

Charlie glanced at his watch. "It's set to blow. We don't know how much time we have. I know it isn't the popular answer, but we wait."

Chapter Thirty-Six

"Oh no!" Laura's eyes went wide as the familiar figure came into view. "Harding."

Myers turned to the monitors and then to Deshawn. "I can hold them out for a while, but if Harding has an override code, that will be it."

"Can we hide?" Laura glanced around the small space. "Let him come in. Get him when he is least expecting it?"

"How many men are with him?" Deshawn asked, stepping between them.

Myers tapped on the screen. "Maybe five total? It's Harding for sure, but I don't know the others."

Myers snapped off the TV.

Deshawn grabbed the empty bottles and wrappers and tossed them in a box.

They only had seconds to figure this out. Each of them peered around the room and at the ceiling, looking for a hiding place. Together, they moved to the only place not seen at the entrance—the bathroom. It was tiny, and the three of them were practically on top of each other, but it was all they had.

Laura angled to the left to free a hand. Part of her left leg was going numb from Myers' body weight. "We have to be able to fight. I don't think this is going work."

"I have an idea." Deshawn walked out of the room.

Laura started to follow him but decided against it when she heard the beeping of the code box. "How long?" she whispered in Myers' ear.

"Two minutes tops." He motioned for her to get in the shower, and she shook her head. "You know I'm the better fighter."

He nodded and pointed to the door.

Laura positioned herself behind it. When they came in, she would have to put them out with a sleeper hold. Anything else, and it would give them away. Even a silencer in this small space would echo. It didn't matter. All she cared about was shooting Harding. After that, the chips could fall wherever they may.

The bunker door slid open. The men filtered in laughing and talking.

"I told you," one deep-voiced male said. "She totally fell for it. Dumb brunette."

"You're just sorry that she—" The room fell silent. Did the men know they were here?

"What are you doing here, Agent Browning?" Harding asked.

"I was told by Operations to report here," Deshawn said coolly. "Something about protecting you. I don't know. I do what I'm told."

"Is that so?"

Steps silently moved through the room. There was no surprise attack. This would be head on. Myers peeked out from the curtain and nodded.

Laura nodded back, pulling a knife from her boot as she readied herself.

The door cracked opened. A boot came into view. Laura waited until he passed her and then slit his throat.

He started to fall forward. Myers caught him and folded him into the shower, while stepping out. Now he was fully exposed.

"Drake?" a guy said outside the door.

Laura pointed to the dead guy.

Myers grunted. "Yeah."

"Is it clear?"

"Yeah. Using it."

Laura carefully twisted the lock as the footsteps moved away. That would allot them a tiny bit more time. The room erupted into talking again. Harding was naturally skeptical, and it was no wonder he came in like that.

"Where's Alicia?" someone asked.

"With the rest." Harding didn't seem concerned.

"You would sacrifice her. I thought she was your girl?"

"You can always get more tail," Harding said. "I was done anyways. She did her job."

Laura grimaced.

The room erupted with laughter, then the TV flicked on. It sounded like sports or something with cheering.

"How long are we down here?" another voice asked.

"Until the coast is clear, and then we'll use the back entrance to the tunnels," Harding said.

Myers mouthed, "Tunnels?"

They were in the back entrance. Together, they began to scan the room, touching each object, fixture, and tile. Laura ran her hand on a wire that led to the back of the toilet. She followed it and yanked slightly. The entire wall started to shift to the left.

Myers quickly flushed the toilet to hide the sound. "You almost done, Drake? I need to duce."

Myers grunted.

The two of them didn't wait. They ran down the tunnel as fast as they could. It was long and dark, but it eventually led to a storm drain. Almost free. They stepped out into the night sky. Medical response lights flashed about ten yards away. They climbed out of the hole and ran for the street. Suddenly, Deshawn flashed through her mind. Would they kill him when they saw she was gone?

"We need to get Deshawn." Laura stopped, out of breath.

"We can't go back in there."

"I will. You get the rest of the team and bring them here." Laura started for the hole, and Myers grabbed her and spun her to face him. "I won't lose you, Laura."

She touched her lips to his and smiled. "You won't. You know that, right?"

"You're good, but there are four guys back there with one thought in their tiny brains—kill Laura Black."

"And one guy here who is going to go get my team and save the day."

He stared at her a moment. "Do not die."

"Yeah, I'll give it my best shot." She ran back into the darkness and toward the bathroom entrance. Maybe the best choice was to go all in. Did she wait for her team or take her chances?

She pulled the body from the shower and laid it in the opening behind the toilet. Someone knocked on the door. "Hurry up, will you?" It was Deshawn.

Laura tried to grunt with a deep voice before

unlocking the door.

Deshawn stepped in.

Laura locked the door, pulled him to the hole, and hissed, "Run."

His eyes shot wide. "What about you?"

"I'm not leaving here without killing Harding."

He stared at her a moment and then nodded. "Then I'll stay."

She shook her head. "My fight. Not yours. Go. Be safe."

Deshawn took a moment to decide, then took off. After a few minutes, another knock came on the door. Laura waited, gun pointed at space. Suddenly, the door kicked in revealing Harding. No hesitation, Laura fired. The bullet hit him in the chest, causing him to fall back. Several goons came around, and Laura shot each one, dead. Within seconds, only Harding breathed.

"So, this is how it ends, huh?" Harding laughed through bloodied teeth.

"I suppose so." Laura changed the ammo on her gun. "It didn't have to be this way, you know."

"You had to know I couldn't just leave you alone to live your life, Black. That isn't how things are done in the agency." He coughed a mouth full of blood, his breath labored.

"You said before we attacked S.I.U. last year that you were going let us go. Now you're saying that was never the case."

"Never the case."

"Why? Why do you want this, Harding? It's vile." She walked in front of him with gun still raised and knelt by his side. "I never wanted any of it. You knew that."

He reached out and touched her face with a bloodied hand. The warm blood felt sticky on contact. "I couldn't let you win, my dear. You left me to rot in this awful place. I couldn't let you wi—." His hand dropped, and all light extinguished from his eyes.

Laura breathed deep. She couldn't believe how she felt. So much pain from this man now left to a pool of blood on the carpet. Tears ran down her face, mixing with his mark. Someone touched her back. She could barely feel it or discern its owner.

"Come on, Laura," came Myers' voice through the cloud.

Explosions rang out above. The ground shook. Dirt shifted. The hole began to collapse around them. Myers swung her into his arms and darted for the entrance. Deshawn was in front of them, running as fast as possible. Chunks of earth fell around them. Twice, Myers tripped but kept moving forward. At the opening, they fell hard to the grassy knoll. Charlie, Eri, Willow, and Teddy all greeted her with relieved smiles plastered on their faces. They had done it. Destroyed the beast.

Chapter Thirty-Seven

Laura climbed in one of the agency vans and settled into one of the back seats.

"I really want to name it," Charlie said for the fourth time.

"It's a standard van. Why does it need a name?" Eri asked, maneuvering into one of the back seats.

"Because then it feels loved and will take care of us." Charlie petted the dashboard on the passenger side. "And we shall forever call her...Bullet."

"Fine, Bullet it is. Can we go now?" Eri slammed the side door closed.

"Yes, let's. Where to now?" Myers asked behind the driver's wheel.

"Yes, but how about we play musical chairs." Charlie got out and joined his wife in back. Shaking her head, Laura climbed around and dropped into the passenger seat next to Myers. "Let's go somewhere very secluded with lots of trees and streams and very few people."

Myers laughed and repositioned the stick shift to reverse. "I like the sound of that."

Teddy leaned forward from the second row of seats. "By the way, we saw Helena and Alicia escape before the explosion. They went with some EMTs in an ambulance."

Laura's heart dropped. "Stop the car!"

Myers touched the brake and turned to her. "What?"

"I will not go into hiding looking over my shoulders anymore. We need to go find them now."

"Shouldn't we rest up first?" Myers touched her hand. "It's been a lot."

"Just one day." She looked over her shoulder at Charlie. "But you find them, and you monitor them. Understood?"

"Aye, aye, Capt'n." Charlie flipped open his laptop and began typing. "I'll have them again momentarily. You can count on me."

"You don't want to wait, do you?" Myers whispered to Laura.

She met his stare. *Of course not.* "What do you think?"

"What has gotten into you today? You're super chipper." Eri eyed Charlie with suspicion.

"I feel relieved. So, sue me." It took a moment before Charlie said, "Okay, got them. Go north."

Myers accelerated and drove down the road onto the freeway.

"Go about two miles, get off at the exit, and turn right," Charlie said.

Myers complied.

"It's that county hospital up there on the left." A six-story beige building came into view. "Pull into the parking garage."

"Wait, I thought you said we were waiting one day?" Teddy asked.

"Yeah, right. Are you sure you've lived with this family for the past year?" Myers drove past the stand, grabbed a ticket, and then parked about three levels up. "One day could mean they are long gone."

"Then why suggest it?" Willow asked.

Laura and Myers exchanged smiles. She didn't answer, just glanced back to Charlie. "Can you detect where they are from here?"

"No, but we could probably guess."

"Emergency," Teddy and Willow said in unison and then laughed.

"Why do you say that?"

Willow leaned forward on the back of the seat with both elbows. "She was pretty torn up."

"Then it's probably a good guess." Laura took a deep breath.

"What should we do?" Myers turned off the ignition and slid to face the group.

"Myers, you and I go in to see if we can find them. Eri, Teddy, and Willow, you stand further out watching the exits, in case they bolt. Charlie, you do you."

Charlie tapped his forehead with two fingers in a salute. "Roger wilco."

Eri raised an eyebrow and exited vehicle.

They each went their separate ways. Laura walked past a car window and saw her reflection. She was a mess—hair stuck up in all directions, ash mixed with sweat smears around her face, dried blood lined the bottom of her nose. "Wait, we need to clean up."

Myers looked somewhat better, but he too looked pretty dirty.

They walked back to the car. Laura grabbed a bottle of water and found some fast food napkins in the glove box. She washed down her face and handed some to Myers to do the same. "Charlie, can Myers borrow your shirt, and can I have your hoodie?"

Charlie laughed. "You think Myers is going to fit my shirt?"

"It'll be snug, but it will look better than what he's wearing now." She looked at the stained olive shirt.

Charlie handed out his black hoodie. Laura pulled it on, as Charlie crawled out of a brown shirt, labeled with some nerd phrase, and gave it to Myers.

Myers held it up. For sure, it would be a size too small. He pulled it on. It was snug, revealing every muscle.

Laura smiled as she smoothed her hair back with the water that was left in the bottle.

"Don't laugh," Myers said

"Who says I'm laughing. Maybe I'm admiring."

He stared at her a moment with an amused grin, then nodded. "Okay, Black. You do you. Let's roll."

"Make sure you have a silencer on your gun."

Myers nodded. "Yeah."

They sprinted back toward the stairwell and skipped down to the bottom level. A red painted arrow on the side of the wall said emergency was to their left. They slowed their pace. Myers grabbed her hand as had always been Laura's advice. Couples were less suspicious.

The emergency room was littered with sick people. A line had formed at the front desks. Laura got in it as she continued to survey the space. Glass, lined with wire, filled one wall. A double door led to the back. A metal button lay on the side of the door, which was guarded by security.

"How do we get in there?" Myers asked.

A front desk person opened up to her right.

"Magic." Laura winked, crossed to the desk, and began to be frantic. Time to channel Teddy. "Excuse me. I just heard my little sister has been brought in. Gun shot to her torso. How could that have happened? She's a good girl. Good grades. No trouble ever. Great friends. Well for the exception of that one boyfriend last year. But he's not in her life anymore."

The woman held up her hand. "What's her name?"

Oh no, there was no way Helena would use her real name. "Try Aneleh Munez," came Teddy's voice. "She used it before. It means something to her."

"Aneleh Munez."

"Yes, you're right. The cops where talking to her, but I think they are finished." The woman clicked on a few buttons. "She is in bed seven. What is your relation again?"

"My sister and that's our stepbrother." Laura glanced at Myers with wide eyes, then back to the lady. "Mack Munez."

"Go to the door, and we'll buzz you through."

Laura moved away and whispered in the com, "Remind me to kiss you later, Teddy."

"I'll take a hot fudge sundae, instead, if that's okay," he replied.

"It's yours."

The two of them walked behind the nurse, through the door, and down a hall. Laura fingered the knife sheaved in her waistband, ready for anything. They reached a sheeted stall at the end of the room, and the nurse stepped back. "She's in here. We've given her something for the pain, so I can't say if she will hear you or not. Please don't stay long."

They both nodded as she moved away.

Laura walked in first and acrimony filled her body at the site of their principal traitor. Helena's eyes were closed and her skin pale. An IV ran from her arm and an air tube was tucked in each nostril. A monitor gauged her vitals.

Myers pulled the pink sheet hanging from the ceiling farther around so they had complete privacy. He then moved to the left side of the bed. Laura walked to the right. An extra pillow lay behind her head. Could they do it here, with all these witnesses around? She glanced at Myers.

He nodded.

She reached for the pillow and pulled it to her chest. This would not be easy. As angry as she was at this woman, she had been her friend. She began to move it forward, when Helena's body shifted.

"I'm sorry," Helena mumbled.

Laura pulled the pillow back. "What?"

"I'm sorry for everything. I know now that Harding killed my dad. I did all that evil for a lie." A tear seeped down her face. "I don't blame you two for hating me. I hate me. But I am sorry."

Tears welled in Laura's eyes. This hurt.

"Do it, please," Helena cried.

"What?" Laura asked.

"What you came here to do. It's okay. You have to."

Laura peered at Myers, unsure how to proceed. They both stood there a long while, no one talking. She couldn't do it. Even though leaving Helena alive would put them all at risk, she didn't know if she could take this defenseless woman's life. Laura placed the pillow back on the bed and stepped back.

"More mercy than I showed Bryce," Helena said.

The mention of his name incensed Laura. Maybe that was why Helena said it. Anger flowed through Laura's veins, but still, she did not reach for the pillow.

"Can I whisper you a secret?"

Laura glanced at Myers, who shook his head.

"I promise, I won't hurt you."

Laura stepped forward, cautiously, and bent down to her side.

"Can you love Myers for me? I took his love. I took yours. And for that, I am sorry. Please take care of him." A quick tug from Laura's knife and Helena sliced her own throat.

Blood sprayed both of them. Laura and Myers stared in disbelief. For a second, she was numb, but then adrenaline kicked in. They had to go. This would look like their doing. Laura grabbed her knife, rubbed it on the side of the sheet, and then hurried to the other exit. She opened the door and gasped. Alicia stood in the stairwell on the phone. Laura didn't hesitate. She reached for her gun and fired. The girl dropped over the railing and down the stairs, crumpling in a pile at the bottom. Luckily, she had put the silencer on.

They took off running, skipping every other step. When they were close enough to the bottom, they leapt over the landing and hit the exit door. An alarm sounded. Not good. The two of them raced across the open parking lot.

"Are you getting this everyone? We have to go!" Laura ran away from the parking garage and down toward a suburb. "Charlie, we can't come to you. You have to come to us. We are on Maple, turning onto Gold." Gasping and holding her side, Laura glanced at

Myers. "You okay?"

He nodded.

They ducked in an alley and ran until it ended in a clump of bushes. She described her location to Charlie and sank down to the earth. Her body shook with too much adrenaline and unbelief.

Myers held her, gasping for breath.

"I am so sorry," Laura cried. Her heart leapt wildly in her chest, and her mind whirled in disbelief. "We are going to be fugitives for the rest of our lives. Normal will never be possible."

"Normal is overrated anyways." He touched his lips to the top of her head. "It'll be okay. *We'll* be okay."

"Before we had anonymity. Now not even that."

"Yeah," he sighed, "but where is the fun in that?"

Sirens sounded in the distance. Both craned their necks to look toward the towering hospital. Time was short. Hopefully, Charlie would get everyone collected and make it out before the place was surrounded. A van screeched to their hiding spot and honked.

The two of them peeked, then jumped from the bushes, got in, and slammed the door shut. The rest of the team stared at them wide-eyed.

"What happened?" Charlie asked, as he sped away.

"Don't go too fast, or it will cause suspicion." Laura used her old shirt from before to wipe her and Myers' faces free of blood splatter. "Helena cut her own throat."

"What?" Eri shook her head. "Of course, she got one last dig in."

"But we got Alicia," Myers said. "So, at least we are free from that standpoint."

"Silver linings," Teddy said sarcastically. "Now what?"

"This is a decision you will all have to make." Laura glanced around at all her friends—her family. Never did she think she could love people so much. "Myers and I are now fugitives—first the viral video and now this. Everyone will know our faces. That life you wanted will not exist for us. We will always be running." Tears pooled in her eyes and trickled down her cheeks. "I will not tell anyone to choose that with us. I actually discourage it. No one knows you. You could have a somewhat normal life if—"

Teddy held up his hand. "Stop. I don't want it."

"What?" She glanced his way.

"Family is where the heart is, correct? Therefore, life is wherever you are." He peered around. "I don't know about you, but I think you'll need us. You won't be able to fend for yourselves."

Laura smirked. "You liked saying that, didn't you?"

Teddy laughed. "Very much."

"The rest of you, I won't—"

"Please," Eri said. "Charlie and I have been with you since the beginning. We're in. Though I want our own cabin."

"That's my girl," Charlie added from the front."

"You know I'm in," Deshawn said.

That left Willow. The girl's face was free of any telling emotions.

"Willow, it won't bother us if you need to go."

Teddy shot Laura an annoyed look. "Speak for yourself, Black." He glanced back at Willow. "What are you thinking? Because I'm thinking I'll go with you if you have to, as long as we can still find them when we miss them."

She slid her hand in his and grinned. "No, I'm in. I was just playing it all out in my head. I'm good. Let's go find the perfect hiding place."

"You heard her, Charlie. Let's go find *our* normal," Teddy said.

Epilogue

A Little Over Two Years Later

The sun slowly rose over the Canadian countryside, casting shadows from the tall moss-covered trees. The air smelt of pine and chimney smoke. Laura stretched on the front porch of her cabin and breathed deep.

Myers came behind her and wrapped a Mexican blanket around her shoulders.

"Good morning, sweetheart." Laura turned and faced her husband. Her heart swelled as he touched his lips to hers. "Have you heard from anyone yet?"

He shook his head. "Charlie promised they'd bring his famous sweet potatoes, so he has to be on time or you know who will be unhappy."

"Yes, there will be some serious yelling. I'm sure you had enough of that already this morning from me. Cooking a turkey in that camp stove was a bit arduous. I hope it tastes okay." She smiled, as a gray bird with a yellow neck flittered to a halt on the railing, pecked at the wood before flying away.

He wrapped his arms around her and whispered in her ear, "How did you sleep last night? More bad dreams?"

She glanced out across their front yard—the view

of thousands of tall trees and only the sounds of nature. It soothed her. She closed her eyes and nodded. Flashbacks and horrible memories had plagued her since they stopped running. Thoughts of death, torture, and all she had seen—it all found a resting place in her unconscious state.

"I hate to be a victim, but we didn't process all of this properly. At S.I.U., we always had to meet with a therapist after a big event. They did most things wrong, but that was one thing they did right." She stared in his eyes. "I think we, or least I, should talk to someone."

"We can't risk it. You know that." He kissed her cheek. "If they rat us out, we're done."

"Aren't they subject to client-patient privilege?"

He shrugged. "Not sure if that includes murder."

The door opened, and little feet pattered to her side. Myers bent down and lifted their daughter onto his left hip. Her blue eyes were reminiscent of Bryce's. One day, Myers and she would explain what happened to her birth daddy, but Myers had filled the position quite well.

"What are you doing out of bed so early, little bug?"

"Hungee."

Myers kissed the top of her black curls. "Me, too. Uncle Deshawn, Uncle Charlie, and Auntie Eri are coming for turkey dinner. How does that sound?"

The toddler nodded her head smiling. "Mashmeyo potatoes."

Laura laughed. "See, that's all you've been talking about and now he better show with the marshmallow potatoes." She reached for her, and Denise filled her arms. The chubby little hands caressed Laura's cheeks.

"Lub mama."

"Yeah, me too." Laura kissed her, just as Charlie's Jeep pulled into the dirt lot below. "Let's get you dressed for Turkey Day, okay?"

"K."

Myers reached for Denise. "I can do it. I think they want to talk to you anyway."

Laura handed over the little girl with a suspicious look. "Why would they want to talk to me?"

Myers winked and disappeared into the cabin with the little girl. Some probably think Denise was a weird choice to name their daughter. But her daughter's blood was Bryce's, so they decided her name could be Denise—giving both their former friends a place in their child's life. The thought made Laura tear up and smile.

Charlie stepped out of the vehicle and walked around to let Eri out as well. She held their prized sweet potatoes in what looked like a casserole dish. Both looked up in unison and waved.

"Hello," Eri yelled up.

"Myers will be so glad you've come bearing that recipe," Laura responded. "He pretends it's for Denise, but we all know better."

"Oh, we know." Charlie took the pan and motioned for Eri to go up the stairs first. Her pregnant frame made her waddle a bit. When they reached the top, Laura took the dish and motioned for them to enter. The house smelled of roasting turkey and baked bread. The fireplace flickered light around the large space filled with woven rugs, a leather couch, and Myers' favorite chair. Charlie went for the chair, knowing full well it would irk his friend. Eri dropped down on the couch and tucked her purse beside it.

"How are you feeling?" Laura asked as she set the sweet potatoes on the stove and then went to join them. Curiosity was getting the best of her. What news could they possibly have? "Are Teddy and Willow okay?"

Charlie nodded. "Yeah, they were able to buy some property about an hour from the border. We can take you some day when it's safe." He exchanged a look with his wife. "Willow still isn't comfortable leaving the states for Canada for some reason. We don't know what that is about, but we're still trying."

So that wasn't the news. Better be outright. "So, Myers said you have news."

The two of them glanced at each other with knowing smiles and then to her.

"Well?"

"I'm pregnant."

Laura laughed. "This I know."

The two exchanged looks again, and then Charlie said, "With twins."

"Congrats!" Laura clapped and stood, crossing to her friend. She hugged her tight, so glad for it to be good news. "I'm so happy for you." She pulled back and touched Eri's stomach. "Oh my gosh! That is so insane."

Charlie stood and walked next to his wife. "I know. We just found out on Friday. We're a bit nervous about the delivery in these conditions, and let's be real, Eri isn't the largest woman."

"Thanks, I think."

Charlie touched her shoulder. "You know what I mean."

Laura understood. All of the trauma of Helena's

abuse had made her labor with Denise a very scary one. It had also been impossible for Laura to get pregnant again. Three miscarriages had made everyone worry. She wanted to go to a regular doctor, but Myers would not allow it. He feared they would be discovered, and all of this would be gone.

They all relaxed on the couch before Eri spoke. "My O.B. had an interesting story to tell. When we explained some of my scars, he unearthed something of interest. He had been abused by S.I.U. for years, before becoming a doctor."

Laura sat up straight. "I'm sorry. S.I.U.?"

"It's okay. He checks out." Charlie glanced at his wife. "Trust me, we panicked at first, too."

"He just so happens to specialize in infertility." Eri shifted forward on the couch. "We would take specific precautions, but we think—"

"Myers would never agree." Laura hated talking about this. From past experience, nothing would happen to change the way things were anyway. Why drudge it up?

"I already have," Myers said from the doorway. "I met him a few weeks ago. We've been following him, tracking him, all to see if we can trust him. We know him pretty well at this point."

Laura stood. "And he seems safe?"

Myers crossed to her and took her hand. "You know I would not allow it any other way."

She hugged him; grateful for all he was to her. "Thank you," she cried.

He kissed her lips and then held her chin softly. "We'll get through this like we do everything else."

Denise came toddling in giggling. She ran to

Charlie and held out her arms. He scooped her up into his lap.

"Mashmeyo Potatoes?"

"You bet, as soon as Uncle Deshawn is here, we'll dig in."

She pointed a chubby finger at the door. "Here."

They glanced out the window. Sure enough, Deshawn walked up the steps with his new girlfriend, Beth. She had checked out as a Canadian hippie who knew nothing about the kind of life they lived. They walked in and hugged everyone. "We brought rolls."

Denise clapped her chubby hands, then dropped back to the floor. "Eat." She tugged on his sleeve. "Eat."

"I couldn't agree more, squirt." Charlie stood and took the little girl's hand, facing Laura. "So, when do we eat?"

Laura laughed. "Give me time to get everything on the table."

Eri joined her. "I'll help."

Beth nodded and followed the women to the kitchenette.

Charlie bent down and looked Denise in the eye. "How about we all help? What do you say?"

"Yes! Yes!" The little girl giggled and ran into the kitchen.

The rest of them followed smiling. They somehow found their normal. It wasn't perfect to some, but it was perfect for a forgotten few.

A word about the author...

Dr. Kimberlee Mendoza works full-time as an adjunct professor and the Director of Instruction at San Diego Christian College. She is also a graphic designer for The Wild Rose Press. She has published more than a fifteen novels and plays and travels around speaking on Generation Z. She resides with her husband and two teenage boys, in San Diego, CA. She has her BA in Human Development, her MA in Humanities, and her Ph.D. in Leadership Studies in Education.